THE SASQUATCH MURDERS

ERIC S. BROWN

SEVEREDPRESS

THE SASQUATCH MURDERS

Copyright © 2025 by Eric S. Brown

WWW.SEVEREDPRESS.COM

ISBN: 978-1-923165-50-2

THE SASQUATCH MURDERS

There was blood everywhere. It smeared the walls and even dripped from the ceiling. The back door of the house, which led into its kitchen, lay in splintered shards and broken fragments. Huge, barefoot tracks could be seen in the congealing red that slicked the floor. Frannie shivered inside the refrigerator. It was cold as hell. The flesh of her naked arms were covered with goosebumps. She rubbed at them, careful not to make any noise as she did. At the moment, the kitchen was quiet, at least as far as she could tell through the fridge's thick walls. Her mother's horrible screams had long since ended. Unable to stop herself, Frannie sniffled. She knew her mom was dead. The monster had torn her apart in a shower of gore. Frannie wasn't sure about her dad.

The three of them had been outside, having a late picnic under the stars, enjoying the warm summer evening when it all started. The whole picnic thing was her dad's idea. He loved watching the night sky and tonight there was supposed to have been some sort of meteor shower that could be seen if you knew where to look, at the right time. . .and of course, her dad did. Amateur astronomy was his passion in life. Her mother loved him enough to go along with most of his celestial oriented adventures. Frannie liked them. They made her father special. None of her friends' dads knew as much about space as him.

Their dinner consisted of thick pattied hamburgers with cheese and homemade fries her mother whipped up. Her father was barely able to contain his excitement as the time of the meteor shower drew closer. Then it came. . .

Their house was remote, far from the streets of town. It was surrounded by woods that stretched for miles in places and onward up into the mountains on the northern side. The monster emerged from the trees. Frannie's father gawked at the thing in disbelief and her mother screamed. The creature was much taller than her father and he wasn't a short man. It wore no clothes, body covered head to toe in brown hair. Half beast, half human, the thing loosed a deep, rumbling growl moving towards them.

"Run!" Frannie's father cried out, swiping her up from where she sat on the spread out picnic blanket. Legs pumping like rapid firing pistons, her father reached the house first. Frannie's mother just wasn't able to keep up with him. Knowing that the house's backdoor would never stop the massive, snarling beast from getting inside, he jerked the fridge open, yanking its inner shelves out.

"Get in!" her father ordered. "And don't make a sound, Frannie. Not a sound, no matter what you hear!"

Nodding to let him know she understood, Frannie climbed into the fridge. Frannie swallowed hard, fighting down a scream, as the door closed and cold darkness engulfed her.

She heard her mother make it into the house and the backdoor slamming. . .then burst apart, exploding inward. Bits of it thumped against the fridge causing Frannie to flinch inside. Pulling her legs even tighter to her chest, Frannie managed not to scream. A shrill shrieking cry of her mother's voice began and was abruptly silenced. It was her father who was screaming then. There was a commotion followed by the sound of impossibly heavy feet thudding across the kitchen floor in the direction of the living room. Frannie knew her father had to be going for his gun in the hallway closet.

Moments later, a shotgun boomed. Frannie waited, expecting another shot, but it never came. Had her father killed the monster? Had it killed him? She shuddered inside the fridge, scared of her own movements. If the monster was still alive and out there, she would be dead too, like her mother, if it found her. Deep down, Frannie knew that her mother was gone and it hurt. All Frannie could do though was stay in the fridge and pray the monster didn't realize she was there.

It was impossible to gauge the passage of time inside the cold darkness of the fridge. The house outside was silent. She hadn't heard anything since the gunshot which could have happened seconds ago or hours. The cold was horrid. It seeped into her bones, chilling Frannie to her core. Each shiver that ran through her small body was accompanied by a fresh wave of terror. She had to keep still. . .she just had to.

Heavy foot steps shook the fridge. The monster had come back. Tears welled up in Frannie's eyes and escaped to slide over her cheeks. She hoped her father had managed to get away from the monster and out of the house but Frannie knew that wasn't what had happened. He would have never left her. She listened as the monster moved about the kitchen. Wet, smacking noises reached her ears. Frannie's hands came up to cover them. They were too sickening to endure. Finally, they stopped. Heavy foot falls thudded across the kitchen again in the direction of the back door and then fell silent. She sat there, crying and whimpering for what seemed like hours.

Frannie knew eventually she was going to have to get out of the fridge or freeze to death. She was so scared to do anything and utterly unsure of what to do. Frannie pressed her ear against the cold door and strained to hear something, anything that might give her a clue as to whether or not the monster was still in the house. There was nothing to be heard though, only silence.

Ever so slowly and gently, Frannie pushed the fridge's door open. The harsh light of the bulb on the kitchen ceiling stung her eyes. She blinked, trying to see better, then looked around. The monster wasn't right outside waiting on her as she feared it might be. Frannie didn't see any sign of the thing. There was a lot of red though, everywhere, flung and splattered about. In that first glance, Frannie's mind refused to let her understand what the red was. When it did hit Frannie, she shrieked like a banshee, tumbling from the fridge onto the blood-slicked floor of the kitchen.

Frannie's mother was in pieces, some crushed and smashed almost beyond recognition. Others were intact but strewn about the kitchen. A strand of her mother's blood-slicked intestines hung from the ceiling fan below the glowing light bulb that lit the room. Frannie had landed right next to one of her mother's severed hands. Wailing, Frannie leaped up and ran out of the kitchen, heading into the living room. As soon as Frannie was through the connecting doorway she saw the monster. It was crouching next to the mutilated corpse of her father. The monster's lips were wet with blood and its left hand clutched a chunk of gnawed upon meat. Realizing where the meat came from, Frannie, unable to stop herself, sprayed hot vomit from her mouth. It shot outward, splattering onto the living room carpet in a stream of bile and partly digested burger and fries.

The monster rose up. Its yellow eyes locked onto Frannie as its lips parted in an inhuman snarl. Flinging the chunk of meat aside, it came bounding towards her. Frannie turned to run, the front of her clothes soaked with puke, and darted back into the kitchen. Frannie knew she couldn't outrun the monster. It was so huge, strong, and fast. She didn't even think about trying to fight it. The fridge door was open. Frannie dived back inside, swinging it closed behind her.

The monster came tearing into the kitchen only to find it empty. Frannie breathed a chilly sigh of relief hearing it stomp on towards and out into the backyard. This time, Frannie promised herself, she wasn't getting out of the fridge again until it was certain that the monster was gone.

****

Across town, Mary Rogers was sitting on her couch. There were no thoughts of the distant and hard to see meteor shower occurring outside in her head. Brandon had gone upstairs to shower. Neither of them were working tomorrow so they had bumped date night up to tonight instead of their usual Sunday evening. Having caused him to work up quite a sweat, Mary was very pleased with herself and riding high on her own afterglow. Clicking through the choices offered by the various streaming services they had, she finally settled on a drama series about a poor housekeeper. Snuggling deeper into the blanket that was on the couch, Mary sighed contently. Life could be really wonderful when it wanted to, she thought.

The TV suddenly cut off, its screen flashing and then going black. Mary cursed, looking around to see it was more than just the TV that had gone out. The power was off. A loud thump sounded upstairs.

"Brandon!" Mary yelled. "You okay?"

He didn't answer. Mary grunted, frustrated by how quickly things could take such an annoying turn. She tossed her blanket aside and got up from the warm, soft spot that had been so comfortable. The air wasn't cold. Fall was close but not here yet and the nights for now continued to be mild. Her steps were slightly hurried as Mary headed for the stairs.

"Brandon!" she called out again. Still, no answer came.

Images of her lover falling in the shower burst into Mary's mind. She could envision his broken neck, head bent sideways at an unnatural angle atop it, blood just barely seeping from his lips. Her Aunt Debbie died in the shower and Mary had been the one to find her body. She'd never fully gotten over that experience. Of course, her aunt had fallen in such a way that her head struck the side of the tub with such force that the elderly woman's skull was cracked open and nose smashed inward. Mary felt sick remembering the sight. Her pace quickened.

"Brandon! Answer me, damn it!" Mary wailed, crying out a third time.

Reaching the top of the stairs, Mary paused there, catching her breath and steadying herself against her inner fears before heading on into the bedroom they shared. It was the connecting bathroom Brandon had gone to. Praying the power would come back on any second, Mary nonetheless paused at the night table next to their bed long enough to snatch up the small, emergency flashlight she kept there. Though small, the flashlight was powerful and Mary blinked her eyes as she clicked it on.

The room, heck, the whole house was eerily silent. Her fear of finding Brandon like she had her aunt all those years ago surged up again, nearly overpowering Mary. A shudder ran through her. Mary's knuckles went white from how tightly she gripped the flashlight. Her thumb and fingers hurt where they pressed on the metal. The pain helped Mary get her focus back. Trembling, she advanced on the bathroom door. It was partly open and creaked on its hinges as Mary drew closer to it.

"Stop screwing around, Brandon," Mary snapped. "This isn't funny!"

No sound or movement came from the bathroom.

Like ripping off a band aid, Mary lunged forward and shoved through the bathroom door. The beam of her flashlight swept directly into the shower and Mary screamed at what she saw there. The shower curtain was torn and in shambles revealing Brandon where he lay. There was a lot of red. On the side of the shower, in its bottom, and on him. Grooves, like claw marks, ran down the length of Brandon's face, cutting through his nose and parting his lips into dangling folds of loose flesh. Mary's shrieking rose in pitch as she saw that his throat was nothing more than a mass of mangled, torn meat. Brandon's hollow, glazed eyes stared up at her.

Mary flung herself around, charging out of the bathroom. As she reached the door of the bedroom that led out towards the rest of the second floor and the stairs, she tripped over her own feet in a frantic state. Mary toppled to the floor, hard, the impact jarring her body. The fall served to break through the state of sheer panic she was in. Though terrified nearly out of her mind, Mary managed to stop wailing. The loud thump, thump, thump, of heavy footfalls approaching her drew Mary's attention to the hall beyond the top of the stairs. Quivering from the depth of her fear, Mary raised her flashlight, shining its beam in the direction of the noise. In its light, she saw the impossible. A massive form was illuminated by the bright beam. It stood over six feet tall, all muscle and hair. The thing's arms drooped at its side, the fingers of its hands ending in long, gleaming talons. Something about the talons didn't look right but Mary was too much in shock and scared to try to make sense of what she saw.

Scrambling to her feet, Mary retreated into the bedroom, slamming its door shut as the creature lunged forward. The hulking beast didn't roar or growl as it came at her and the door closed between them. She wasn't able to stop the beast though. Its brute strength and sheer weight shoved the door inward. Mary stumbled backwards as the beast entered, frantically attempting to dial 9-1-1 on her cell. She managed to make the call but the phone dropped from Mary's trembling hands onto the carpet as she realized no one would be able to reach the house in time to help. Her breaths were ragged gasps, vision blurring, yet Mary refused to just give up on life. She was determined that this thing, whatever the hell it might be, wasn't going to kill her like it had Brandon. Mary sprinted for the closet. Its flimsy door wasn't going to save her from the monster but the pistol

Brandon kept there might. The pistol was an old thing, left to Brandon by his grandfather. The pistol was always loaded and ready though well hidden, tucked away inside a box gathering dust. Mary made it into the closet, jumping up to grab the box which held the weapon. She yanked away its lid, jerking the pistol out. Despite her adrenaline-fueled speed, the thing was faster. Thick arms closed around her body from behind, knocking the pistol from her grasp. It fell onto the carpet at Mary's feet as the hair-covered arms closed even tighter, as if attempting to crush her rib cage. Kicking and screaming, Mary fought to break free from the beast's bear hug. Her hands reached back, fingernails clawing at the beast's face and neck as her feet slammed into the front of its legs, over and over. With a deep grunt, the beast lurched away, releasing her. Mary dove for the pistol. The beast, already recovered, swiped at her with a taloned hand. Mary squealed, blood spurting from the wounds that they opened up on her back. It was like fighting Freddy Krueger, she thought.

Mary landed on the carpet. Her right hand closed on the butt of the pistol as she rolled over to aim it upwards at the beast. A huge, hair-covered hand slapped the pistol sideways as Mary squeezed its trigger. The bullet punched into the wall near the closet door. The beast took hold of her again, hauling her up from the floor, and flinging Mary across the bedroom. She slammed into the opposite wall and bounced off it, landing roughly on her left shoulder. Mary yelped, feeling it dislocate inside its socket. The beast pounced onto her, slicing her with the talons of one hand and then the other as she screamed at the top of her lungs. Blood flew and flesh separated each time its talons made contact with her body. The last of Mary's strength waned and left her. Her arms fell aside as the beast leaned closer over her and rammed its talons into her throat. They sunk so deep their tips emerged from the back of her neck. Mary bucked and jerked, staring up into the beast's fury filled brown eyes. They were the last thing Mary saw before her world went black.

****

"Damn," Sheriff Clark whispered, shaking his head. He was no stranger to gory crime scenes but this one took the proverbial cake. Frank, his lead deputy, had warned him but he hadn't really believed how bad things were until stepping into the kitchen of the house himself. The poor woman who lay near the backdoor looked like she'd swallowed a grenade and it had detonated inside her. There were bits of her everywhere. Worse, many of those bits looked like they had been partially eaten, as if something had been gnawing on them.

"There's more," Frank said. "Got a dead guy, likely her husband, in the living room too."

Sheriff Clark could tell that Frank was holding something back. He stopped in the kitchen, glancing at the deputy. "And?"

"You won't believe what's in the fridge," Frank stepped to open its door.

"God have mercy," Sheriff Clark said as he saw the girl. She couldn't have been more than twelve years old. The girl's skin was blue which made it very clear that she had frozen to death inside the fridge.

"She wasn't stuck in there," Frank moved the door of the fridge on its hinges showing him how easily the door opened and closed. "This is a newer fridge, not like the deathtraps they used to make when we were kids. That kid could have gotten out anytime she wanted, Sheriff. The question is, why didn't she?"

That didn't take a genius to figure out.

"She hid in there," Sheriff Clark said, "and was so damned scared that she opted to freeze to death rather than try to make a run for somewhere safe."

"Yep," Frank nodded in agreement. "Poor kid. She had to have heard everything going on out here. Can you imagine listening to your parents being torn up like this?"

The kitchen of the house was silent for a moment as Sheriff Clark took a longer, better look around where he stood.

"What are you thinking?" Frank asked.

"Animal attack," Sheriff Clark answered. "Something big got into the house, something ticked off and hungry. . . a bear maybe."

Even as he said the words, Sheriff Clark couldn't bring himself to fully believe them. He'd never seen anything like this mess in his entire career. Besides, bears didn't usually go after humans, much less follow them into their home to slaughter them in a well lit kitchen. He couldn't rule out a bear attack at this point though. Anything was possible and something like that was the only thing he could think of that remotely made any sense.

"Then how do you explain the footprints?" Frank pointed at one on the kitchen floor near where they stood.

Sheriff Clark cocked an eyebrow at the deputy before looking where Frank directed his gaze. He blinked. What the hell?, Sheriff Clark wondered and moved to kneel down next to the smeared mark on the red-slicked floor. The thing looked like it was made by a barefoot giant. The print was far larger than Clark would have thought could be made by a human yet it was much closer in shape to that of a man's than an animal's.

"They're damn big, I'll say that," Sheriff Clark shrugged as he rose back to his feet. "Not sure what to make of them though. I can't see any human making this kind of mess."

Frank chuckled. "No hulking mutated cannibals, huh?"

Sheriff Clark managed a weak grin at the deputy's attempt at a joke.

"Not in these parts," Sheriff Clark shook his head and walked out of the kitchen into the adjoining living room where the other body was. The man's corpse wasn't as utterly torn apart as the woman's but was still a ghastly sight. Both of the man's arms were bent backwards with the white of bone poking through flesh at their snapping points. His stomach had been opened up and looked to have been dug into by something. Strands of intestine that appeared to have been bitten in two spilled over the sides of his abdomen. Sheriff Clark checked out his feet. Not only were they too small to have made the tracks in the kitchen but the man was wearing shoes.

"Guy tried to put up a fight from the looks of it," Frank commented from the doorway behind him.

Sheriff Clark saw what Frank meant. A shotgun, barrel bent and stock nearly completely smashed lay on the living room floor. Picking it up, he could tell that the weapon had been fired.

"Nothing about all this adds up," Sheriff Clark said more to himself than Frank. "Just what in the hell did happen here?"

Daryl came running into the kitchen shouting, "Sheriff! Sheriff!"

"Whoa!" Frank shouted, spinning towards him. "Careful!"

Daryl slipped in the blood that was everywhere in the kitchen, his feet flying out from under him. He crashed onto the floor.

Sheriff Clark stormed through the doorway, marching himself up to tower above Daryl. "That was evidence you just destroyed, son," he said seeing that the young deputy had wiped away the footprints with his fall. The blood they had been left in was now all over Daryl's backside.

Daryl stared up at him, sputtering as he tried to speak. "S-s-sorry."

"Damn," Frank grunted.

"I. . .I . . .I just had to tell you, Sheriff," Daryl blurted out.

"Tell me what?" Sheriff Clark offered the young deputy a hand, helping him to his feet.

"There's been another killing," Daryl stammered.

"What?" Sheriff Clark's eyes went wide.

"On the other side of the town," Daryl spat. "At the Rogers' house. Somebody murdered both of them."

Hillston was a small town where most folks knew each other. Sheriff Clark not only knew the Rogers' first names but could call up images of Mary and Brandon's faces in his mind. It was insane. There hadn't been a murder in the town for years and now, two in one night?

"Who's over there?" Sheriff Clark barked.

"Derrick and Clay," Daryl answered.

Frowning, Sheriff Clark turned to Frank. "I need to get over there. You got things in hand here?"

"You know it," Frank assured him.

Without another word, Sheriff Clark walked out of the house, heading for his patrol car in the driveway beyond it. As soon as he got in it, Sheriff Clark reached for the radio.

"Becca," he said, "This is Sheriff Clark.

Where's Hannah?"

"She's on patrol in town, sir," Becca responded. "Everyone else is either with you or over at the Rogers' house."

"Tell her to head over there A.S.A.P.," he ordered, already cranking up the car.

"Copy that," Becca said.

The wheels of his patrol car sent gravel flying as Sheriff Clark threw the vehicle into reverse, backing out of the drive, and then peeled out, darting down the road towards the other side of town, blue lights flashing and sirens blaring.

****

Clay stood on the porch of the Rogers' house. Raising his palms to cover his mouth and nose, he exhaled into them, trying to see if he could still smell alcohol on his breath. Clay was really knocking back the beers before the crap hit the fan in Hillston and every available officer had been ordered to come in. Clay knew that he shouldn't have reported in, given his current questionable state of soberness, but needed the extra hours on the clock too badly to sit things out. Thankfully, all he could smell was bile. He and Derrick had both vomited after seeing the bodies of the husband and wife inside. Clay opted to stay outside after that, making sure that if the press or anyone showed they couldn't get in to disrupt the crime scene.

The screen door creaked as it opened and Derrick joined him on the porch.

"You get all the pictures you needed?" Clay gestured at the phone still clutched tightly in Derrick's right hand.

"Yeah," Derrick sounded pretty shaken up. "Yeah, I think so."

Clay watched Derrick shove the phone into the pocket of his uniform and trade it for a pack of smokes. Derrick pounded a cigarette loose from the pack and lit up.

"What do we do now?" Clay asked.

"Keep the scene secure and wait for Sheriff Clark I reckon," Derrick took long, deep drags on his cigarette as they talked. "Nothing else we can do."

"So we don't have to go back in there?" Clay gestured at the house's front door.

"Nope," Derrick said.

"Thank God for that," Clay let out a sigh of relief.

An SUV came up the street, pulling into the house's drive.

"What the hell?" Derrick flung the butt of his cigarette away, starting down the steps from the porch. Clay was already down them and in the yard, walking briskly towards the SUV.

"Hey!" Clay shouted. "You can't park that here!"

The SUV's driver side door swung open and a man dressed in a black, expensive looking suit got out. The man was in his early forties as far as Clay could tell. He was fit and moved with a confidence that was almost scary. There was a lethal air about him. Clay suddenly felt that yelling at the man like he had maybe wasn't the smartest move on his part.

The man in black flashed a badge at him.

Clay froze in his tracks. "You're FBI?"

"Agent Trystan Burke," the man snapped, looking him over. "Where's your sheriff at, Deputy?"

"He's not here yet," Derrick cut in before Clay could say anything. "He's on his way though."

"I'll be taking over here, Deputy," Agent Burke said. "My task force is en route."

"I don't think Sheriff Clark is going to care too much for that." Derrick hopped down from the porch, approaching Agent Burke and Clay.

"Nonetheless," Agent Burke shrugged. "That's what is going to happen. Now, if you'll excuse me, I'd like to take a quick look around the scene before my forensics crew arrives."

"Whoa," Clay moved to block Agent Burke's path. "You can't go in there. The sheriff told us not to let anyone in until he gets here."

"Deputy," Agent Burke glared at him, "I highly suggest you move aside."

"Better do as he says," Derrick warned Clay.

Scowling worriedly at Agent Burke, Clay stepped aside.

"Thanks," Agent Burke grinned at the two of them. "I'll be inside. Send your sheriff on in when he gets here."

Derrick and Clay watched Agent Burke head on into the Rogers' house.

"What the hell do you make of that?" Derrick asked Clay, not really expecting any kind of real answer. Derrick was well aware that his friend wasn't the sharpest tool in the shed.

Clay just shook his head. "Guy's a jerk. I hope the sheriff tears him a new one."

"Clay, that's not what I meant," Derrick sighed, lighting up another cigarette. "I meant how in the hell did he even know about what happened in there, man? It's not like it's been on the news yet. Hell, other than the neighbors here and a few passers-by no one knows."

In an unlikely moment of intelligence, Clay said, "Maybe he has a scanner and was listening in on our radios. He'd know all the codes."

Derrick was impressed. "I bet you're right. It's the only thing explains how he knew. Still doesn't explain why he'd be listening in though or what he's doing in our town."

"Ah hell, man," Clay frowned. "Here comes the sheriff. Let him figure all that crap out."

Sheriff Clark's patrol had its lights flashing but sirens turned off as it pulled over on the side of the street behind Agent Burke's SUV. He got out, anger burning in his eyes, and marched up to them.

"Who the frag is that?" Sheriff Clark demanded to know, "And why are they parked in front of my crime scene?"

"FBI, sir," Derrick answered. "Agent by the name of Burke. Told us he was taking over here and to stay out of the way."

"What?" The rage in Sheriff Clark's eyes grew more intense. "And you just let him go on in there?"

"He had identification," Derrick said. "What could we do?"

Two vehicles came roaring along the road, pulling up to where the patrol cars and the SUV were parked. They, too, were black SUVs. What was clearly a forensics crew emerged from one as a pair of well dressed women got out of the other.

The forensics crew headed for the house without even bothering to acknowledge Sheriff Clark and his deputies. The two female agents, they had to be FBI, marched straight towards them though. One was tall and heavily muscled with dark hair pulled tightly up into a pony tail. The other woman was of average height and nowhere near as stocky in her build, hair dark red and cut short.

"Sheriff," the tall woman greeted him. "I'm Agent Seymour and this is Agent Owens."

Forcing himself to control the anger raging within him, Sheriff Clark stared at the odd pair a moment before speaking. "This is my crime scene."

"No Sheriff, it's not, not anymore," Agent Owens corrected him.

"Agent Burke is in charge here now," Agent Seymour added.

"No," Sheriff Clark argued, keeping his voice level. "This is my town, my people who were killed here, you're not cutting me out."

"Sheriff, you've got to understand that. . ." Agent Owens began.

Agent Burke came out of the Rogers' house interrupting her. "Ease off, Owens. No one is cutting anyone out, Sheriff. In fact, I think we both need all the help we can get."

"That so?" Sheriff Clark eyed Agent Burke.

"It is," Agent Burke nodded.

"You wanna explain how you got here so quickly?" Sheriff Clark asked.

"Sure," Agent Burke spread his arms in a showy gesture of submission. "The man who killed the people in this house, Sheriff, I've been chasing him for months. His name, as best we can tell, is Manford Page. These aren't his first victims. Far from it. Manford has left a trail of corpses from the Bread Basket to your town. This bastard isn't just another serial killer, Sheriff. This sicko likes to dress up like Bigfoot when he stalks his prey."

"You're freaking kidding me," Sheriff Clark scoffed.

"I'm not," Agent Burke told him, "I'm deadly serious. Manford literally dresses up like a Sasquatch and kills his victims in such a fashion that some of the murders have actually been thought to be animal attacks by officers who were, shall we say, a bit lazy on their jobs. That is until we discovered what was really going on and started putting all the pieces together."

"That doesn't explain how you knew his next victims would be in my town," Sheriff Clark challenged Agent Burke.

"We've been monitoring the radio chatter of

the law enforcement agencies in this area and around it. As luck would have it, we were passing through your county and overheard about the murders in this house," Agent Burke explained.

Sheriff Clark wasn't happy about the FBI listening in on him and his people. They surely had clearance on some high level to do so. He wondered just how high of a level.

"I'm curious then, why the Rogers house here and not the other scene across town?" Sheriff Clark dug a pack of tobacco from his pocket and shoved some into his cheek.

Agent Burke blinked and shot a frustrated glance towards Owens and Seymour.

Sheriff Clark spat dark brown juice into the grass and laughed out loud. "You didn't catch that one, did you?"

"No Sheriff, I suppose we didn't," Agent Burke frowned. "Guess we missed that one."

"Well then, I'm sure you'd like to know we got a whole family dead too," Sheriff Clark said. "Little girl froze to death in a refrigerator rather than come out of it after hiding there. Her parents were torn apart and partly eaten. Dad at least tried to put up a fight, for all the good it did him."

"Eaten?" Agent Burke frowned.

"Yeah, I was thinking the mess might have been an animal attack until you showed up and told me about your guy," Sheriff Clark spat out more tobacco juice. "He's a cannibal too, huh?"

"No," Agent Burke shook his head. "There's been no evidence of that so far. We're gonna need to pay a visit to that scene too, Sheriff, after my people are done here."

Weighing his options, Sheriff Clark took a step towards Agent Burke. "Look, I realize you've got jurisdiction here, Agent Burke. All I'm asking is to work together, for my people not to be cut out. This is my town and the folks here depend on me to keep them safe. It's my responsibility."

Seeming to consider what he'd said for a moment, Agent Burke finally nodded, "I think that would be a good idea, Sheriff. Like I said, I think we are both going to need all the help we can get."

Agent Burke extended his hand and Sheriff Clark shook it.

****

Leaving his crew at the Rogers' house, Agent Burke, accompanied by Agent Owens, followed Sheriff Clark to the other murder scene. The sun was coming up, its early rays breaking through the darkness. Deputies Frank and Daryl were waiting outside for them when they arrived. Two ambulances were parked nearby too. On the way over, Sheriff Clark had touched base with Hannah over the radio and filled her in on everything going on. She'd arrived at the Rogers' house and joined Burke's people there.

"We ain't moved anything," Daryl informed Sheriff Clark as he and the agents approached the house.

Sheriff Clark heard Agent Owens mutter something about the young deputy under her breath, ignoring it, as he led the way into the house.

Flies and the smell of death greeted the trio as they stepped into the kitchen. Agent Owens actually flinched at the sight. Sheriff Clark watched Agent Burke slowly taking everything in. . .then the lead agent abruptly knelt to closer examine a piece of the dead woman's body that lay close to where he stood.

"Your guy is one sick. . ." Sheriff Clark was saying but stopped as Agent Burke raised a hand at him.

"Show me the rest," Agent Burke ordered.

Sheriff Clark did, taking him to the man's body in the living room and then returning to the kitchen to open the fridge door, revealing the little girl inside. The two agents studied it all closely. Agent Owens kept her mouth shut. He figured she didn't want to comment on anything at all until hearing what her boss had to say about it. Sheriff Clark understood that, though his patience was wearing thin. These people had just rolled into *his* county and taken over. Jurisdiction or not, it didn't feel right.

"Okay," Sheriff Clark said, "You've had your look, now I want you tell me how in the hell your guy did that to the kitchen door."

He gestured at the scattered and broken pieces which had exploded inward as whoever or whatever killed the family forced their way through it. "I don't care how big and strong your psycho is, I ain't never met a human who could do that kind of damage."

Agent Burke didn't respond to his statement, instead, bending over and reaching out with a gloved hand to touch the little girl in the fridge. Sheriff Clark could see the pain in the FBI man's eyes. He knew the feeling well.

"Still waiting on you to explain the door to me, Agent Burke," Sheriff Clark said, wanting to take Agent Burke's mind away from the guilt he appeared to be taking onto himself more than he actually wanted an answer.

Then it hit him like a ton of bricks. Sheriff

Clark exclaimed, "Damn! None of this fits with your guy, does it?"

Agent Burke met his eyes. "It does and it doesn't."

"What in the devil is that supposed to even mean?" Sheriff Clark demanded.

"This certainly fits the way Manford strives for with his kills. . ." Agent Burke's eyes moved around the kitchen, "But even as violent and depraved as he is, I'm not sure how Manford managed this because you're right, Sheriff. That door and the state of the man and woman here, especially the woman, seem beyond. . ."

"What a man could do," Sheriff Clark finished for him. "You should know, there were prints here, Burke. Prints way larger than a man could make too. One of my deputies fell and smeared them but take my word for it, they were huge and weird as hell."

"That's normal for Manford," Agent Burke almost looked relieved at the news of them. "He always tries to leave prints behind. It's part of his psychosis."

"Your poser Sasquatch?" Sheriff Clark grinned. "Out there trying to make people believe. I'll admit that makes a hell of a lot more sense than the monster he's playing at being really walking around killing people. Faking tracks is easy. So is dressing up like a monster. Busting apart a heavy door like the one lying in bits all over this kitchen or tearing up people with your bare hands ain't, though."

"Could be Manford's found a means of boosting his level primal savagery. He could have taken some kind of drug that. . ." Owens tried to offer in way of explanation.

Sheriff Clark wasn't buying it. "You really saying that a hit of some stims gave him the strength to do all this?"

"I am saying that Manford's smart, Sheriff," Owens' expression was grim and deadly serious. "As crazy as he is, the man's a genius when it comes to killing."

"Can't argue that," Sheriff Clark said in an almost mocking tone, gesturing at the bits of the door again. "That's pretty damn impressive."

"I don't have all the answers yet, Sheriff, but I will. I promise you that," Agent Burke frowned. "Unfortunately for you and yours, Manford will most likely kill again in this area before moving on. He's had too much success here not to."

"The upside is that with your help we just might be able to figure out where before it happens," Owens grinned.

****

Manford Page was indeed a large man. His GMC Yukon was supposed to be one of the best vehicles on the market for big people yet even so Manford had needed to modify it himself so that he could fit comfortably in the driver's seat in his second skin. Other people might simply call what he wore a costume but that wouldn't do it justice. Manford had made every inch of the suit himself. Its only imperfection was around the eyes. He'd never been able to get that part as close to the look he was after, no matter what he did. Though Manford wore yellow contacts that resembled an animal's eyes when he was inside the suit and it still didn't seem enough.

He clutched the Yukon's steering wheel tightly, careful not to cut into it with his "claws" waiting for the sun to go down. After killing his last victims, Manford found himself hungry for the thrill of murdering a few more before leaving the area. Finding the closest campground, Manford drove through it as the sun was rising to study its layout and see what he could find out about those who were dwelling there. Then Manford headed back down the road until he found a secluded spot nearby to park the Yukon so that it couldn't be seen by passers-by. Only then had Manford allowed the exhaustion he felt to overtake him, spending most of the day asleep in the driver's seat with the doors of the Yukon locked. In the late afternoon, he had awoken and began to plan out the hunt for his next victims.

As soon as darkness fully fell, he would go prowling through the woods in search of his next prey. Manford always hoped that one day when he killed in a remote area like this one that maybe, just maybe, there would be one of his own kind out here. Manford's mother swore that his father had left them when he was just a baby, too young to remember, but he knew the truth of things. His father wasn't a human but rather a Sasquatch that had raped her in the woods beyond their backyard. That was why she was afraid of those woods until the day the cancer took her to the grave.

Everyone Manford found the courage to tell the truth about his father to had always thought that he was insane, crazy, merely unable to deal with being abandoned. He wasn't though. Manford explored those woods surrounding his childhood home throughout his entire youth and while he'd never been able to locate the beast that was his father, there was plenty of evidence of it in terms of tracks and spore. He'd never given up searching for his kind and never planned to. Manford knew Sasquatch were real and one day, after finally finding them, they would be his family. In the meantime, those who abused nature, denied their existence, and were unkind, would die in their name. Blood would run until the world knew and accepted the truth about he and his kind.

Shaking his head to chase away such human thoughts, Manford looked out through the Yukon's windshield. The long shadows among the trees were deep and dark now. Night had arrived and it was time for the hunt to begin. Easing open the door, Manford emerged from the Yukon, closing it with equal care behind him. The interior lights never came on during that process. He had long ago rewired them to be completely manual in their operation.

Manford stretched, popping his back, and stood straight up to his full six foot seven height. Inside his second skin suit, his body was all hardened muscle. Manford put a lot of effort into being the strongest, toughest possible version of himself that he could be. The metal of the suit's claws gleamed in the early starlight. Flexing his hands, Manford readied his mind for what was to come. Soon there would be screams and blood.

The campground was to the north and he moved in that direction as quietly as a beast of the forest itself might. Manford had scoped it out before choosing the place. Only a handful of what were likely families and couples were staying there, one of them in an RV parked right next to the campground's edge where its borders met the woods.

The darkness of the night became nearly complete as clouds gathered above blotting out the moon and stars. The air felt like rain was on its way. That didn't matter to Manford. His mind was keenly focused on the pleasure of the task at hand. He reached the tree line, stopping among its shadows, peering into the campground. The camper he'd chosen as his target remained distant from the two others. Its lights were out. Beneath the hideous, bestial face of his second skin, Manford's lips drooped in a frown. He had so much more fun when his prey was awake. It went against everything within him to kill someone while they slept. There was just no sport or challenge in that. Any fool could do it.

The campground was quiet and still. Manford crept from the trees, approaching the camper. Though the feet of his second skin were huge, they made very little noise as he walked across the grass. Getting inside wouldn't be a problem. He had several options even if the door was locked. The claws of his second skin could easily be used to pick a lock and, of course, failing that, Manford was more than strong enough to go straight through it.

Reaching the camper, Manford saw the two steps below its door. Now they might be a problem. As soon as he put his weight on them, the camper would surely be jostled by his weight and the steps would creak, alerting anyone awake within to his presence. A good number of people who camped like this brought guns with them. Sometimes no more than a pistol but a shotgun or rifle was more than he wanted to deal with. Under normal circumstances, Manford admitted to himself that he would have watched the camper and its occupants more before making his move. The couple Manford had slain in town left him on such a high, he was seeing red, bloodlust nearly out of control. He was going in pretty much blind so this needed to be fast and brutal.

Manford smashed his way inside. The door burst inward, hinges popping. There was someone sleeping in what passed for the living room. The young man there came awake, eyes bugging wide at the sight of Manford in his second skin. Launching himself up from the couch, the young man tried to make a run for the hallway that led deeper into the camper.

Manford was on him before the fellow had made it more than a few feet, the claws of his second skin raking down the young man's back. The pain of the wounds drove the young man to turn around, facing him. Blood splattered onto the walls as Manford's claws sliced open his neck. Hands coming up to clutch what was left of it in a desperate and vain attempt to stop the blood flow, the young man stumbled backwards, dropping to his knees. Manford gave the dying young man a final slap, knocking him aside, before loosing a thunderous roar and charging down the hallway towards the rear of the camper.

Noises came from the room at the end of the hallway which could only be a small bedroom. The door leading into it was a flimsy thing and didn't even slow him down. Crashing into the room, another young man with blonde hair was there, swinging a baseball bat in an arc towards Manford's face. One of his huge, hairy hands caught it as a teenage girl shrieked like a banshee on the other side of the bed from where he and the young man fought.

"Scott!" she wailed as Manford jerked the baseball bat free of his grasp and flung it aside.

Bone crunched as Manford's fist slammed into Scott's nose. Blood splashed as Scott was knocked over onto the bed. Manford fell on top, one hand swiping through the air after the other, over and over, flinging blood as the razor sharp blades that were the claws of his second skin ripped the kid apart. Scott's guts opened up, spilling out in red-slicked, purple strands onto the white sheets. A streak of perverted pleasure coursed through Manford as one of his hands grabbed Scott by the groin, claws sinking in, deeply. Scott wailed like a stuck pig, eyes rolling up, and died.

Manford's huge form was blocking the only way out of the bedroom. Its side window was too small for the girl to escape through. There was nowhere for her to go but at him. Lacking the nerve for that, the girl, continuing to scream, tried to keep the bed and the body of her dead lover between them. The ceiling was too low for Manford to go bounding over the bed and the room was so cramped he couldn't just throw it from his path either. Ducking his shoulders and head, Manford brought up a knee onto the side of the bed, leaning to make a grab at the girl. He wouldn't have thought it possible but somehow her voice rose in pitch again. Pressing herself flat against the wall behind her, the girl was able to avoid him getting hold of her. Knowing he needed to shut the girl up, Manford lunged forward again, most of his weight now atop the bed.

The girl had been playing him, Manford realized, as she whipped out a lighter and can of hairspray from the small closet next to her. Whipping them up and aiming the spray at his eyes, her thumb flicked the lighter. Manford drove sideways as a blast of fire erupted, whooshing through the air. Though he managed to save himself from being caught in the face by it, the flames still lit his shoulder on fire. Manford awkwardly withdrew from the bed. His hair-covered left hand came up to slap out the fire on his right shoulder. Now he was really damn mad. The girl shot another blast in his direction but Manford had withdrawn beyond its reach. Spotting the baseball bat on the floor, he snatched it. With every ounce of his strength, Manford threw it at the girl. The bat struck her skull with enough force to crack it. The girl thudded back against the room's wall and slumped down to collapse onto the floor. It wasn't the sort of kill that Manford preferred or even wanted. The wrongness of it disgusted Manford, leaving an almost physical bad taste in his mouth. Giving a displeased snort, he ducked out the bedroom doorway.

As Manford paused to look back at the

sprawled out and mutilated corpse of the girl's lover on the bed, his real lips stretched into a feral smirk beneath those of his second skin suit. The evening hadn't been completely wasted. Scott, if that was really his name, had put up a decent struggle and his friend in the living room had added to the fun.

In the corner of his eye, Manford caught sight of something flickering outside the camper. He turned his head to see a pair of sheriff patrol cars and a black SUV pulling up. Their sirens weren't on, only their lights. Someone in the campground must have heard the girl's distant screams, noticed the camper shaking during his fight with her, and called for help.

The SUV had to be either SBI or FBI. Manford gritted his teeth and then snarled, knowing he couldn't fight that many cops and agents. Tongue flicking over his teeth, Manford watched them getting out of their vehicles. Roaring like the beast he was in his own mind Manford charged the camper's back door. It gave way as he plunged out. Voices cried out in warning at the sight of him. His sharp ears heard the sound of weapons being readied. Some of those same voices began to yell for him to stop. Manford had no intention of doing that. His long legs pumped beneath him, like the chugging pistons of an engine, as he ran full out for the cover of the close by trees. A gunshot rang out, then another. Splinters of bark erupted from the trunk of a tree to his right as Manford reached the woods, a bullet striking it. It didn't matter. He was in the shadows now. He was home.

****

"Damn it!" Agent Seymour shouted. "We can't let the bastard get away."

Manford was already bounding away through the woods.

The local deputies accompanying her were firing at him, spraying the tree line with lead. Agent Seymour couldn't blame them, having taken a hurried shot at the freak herself as soon as she was out of her SUV and saw him. And he was a freak. She'd known that but seeing Manford, in his suit, in real life, wasn't something that Agent Seymour was ever going to forget.

Manford seemed even larger than his file made him out to be. The suit he wore was scary in its realism. The thing appeared to be made out of actual hair and skin. From what. . . she didn't know or want to.

The deputies with her, Hannah and Derrick, stopped firing and sprinted towards the tree line in pursuit of Manford. She considered letting them go and heading into the camper to see if there was anyone alive inside. Her gut told her that there wasn't. Agent Seymour's eyes ran the length of its exterior looking for any sign of life anyway.

A fresh burst of gunfire from the woods made up Agent Seymour's mind for her. She took off in the direction they'd come from, calling Agent Burke as she ran.

"We've found Manford!" Agent Seymour yelled. "He's heading into the woods surrounding the Green Grove Campground!"

Agent Seymour charged through the trees, heart pounding, not having a clue where in the hell the two deputies were or which way to go. The gunshots had fallen silent. Not wanting to risk giving away her location in case Manford was close by, Agent Seymour didn't call out to the two deputies, figuring that she might just get lucky and nail the freak herself. Switching how she held her pistol to a two handed grip, she kept moving forward but slower now, pace cautious and careful, listening to the sounds around her.

Despite her efforts, Agent Seymour wasn't used to navigating wooded areas in the dark. A twig snapped under her feet and she flinched as if it were a detonating bomb.

"Damn," Agent Seymour muttered, voice no louder than a whisper. Allowing a moment to pass in order to both make sure the sound hadn't brought any attention to her and to recenter herself, Agent Seymour started moving again.

She crept through the woods. Their shadows deepened as with each step she took the few lights of the campground grew more distant. As she rounded the side of a large tree, Agent Seymour bit her lip to keep from screaming. She might be a professional but that didn't make her more than human. Hannah's limp form was slumped against its trunk. The deputy's face was little more than shreds of sliced meat that dangled loosely, barely clinging to the white bones of her face. Manford had cut her up badly. What he had done to the deputy was vicious and sickening. And he hadn't stopped at her face either. The sick bastard had cut into Hannah's chest and popped the deputy's rib cage apart. An unbeating heart steamed in the cool air of the night before Agent Seymour's eyes. With a start, she realized just how close Manford must be. She likely scared him away before he was done mutilating Deputy Hannah's body or the woman's heart wouldn't still be where it was.

Was Derrick dead too? Was she alone with Manford? Agent Seymour didn't have a damn clue. Wishing she had stayed in the campground and waited for backup to arrive, Agent Seymour backpedaled carefully away from Hannah's corpse. She sucked in a deep breath.

"Hey!" Derrick shouted, appearing from the shadows.

The deputy's face drained of blood, instantly going pale, as Agent Seymour's pistol came up, aimed at his face.

"Whoa!" he yelled. "It's me!"

Agent Seymour was scowling at him as she lowered her gun. "I nearly put a bullet in your brain, Deputy."

"I saw," Derrick agreed.

"Don't they teach you cops anything anymore?" Agent Seymour grumbled.

"Well, technically I ain't a cop," Derrick pointed out.

Agent Seymour huffed in frustration.

Derrick was staring at Hannah's corpse.

"Oh frag me," he muttered. "That bastard got Hannah."

"Yeah," Agent Seymour could see how he was beginning to really freak out. "I suggest we get the hell out of these woods and wait for backup, Deputy."

Derrick nodded frantically, "Yes ma'am. I think that's a good idea."

He moved towards Hannah, kneeling as if about to try to pick her body up.

Agent Seymour shook her head. "Leave her for now."

"But. . ." Derrick frowned.

"Leave her," Agent Seymour said again more firmly. "Manford is still out here. We can't let the bastard catch us in a state where we aren't both ready to fight back."

"I get it," Derrick said, "I don't like it but I get it."

He rose to his feet and the two of them headed back towards the campground together.

****

The beer tasted like crap. Jerry, honestly, didn't want it. Sym and Caleb were chugging theirs down. All of them were underage. They shouldn't be having any at all but Caleb had broken into his old man's stash and stolen an entire six pack. And to Sym, that made Caleb a hero. Out here, this deep in the woods, there was no worry of getting caught.

The three of them were out here as often as their parents and school would allow. The one thing they had in common were dirt bikes and the nearby trail was the best to ride in the county. Caleb was the daredevil, always taking crazy risks and doing dangerous stunts, Sym was the casual enthusiast who simply loved the experience of the ride, while Jerry was the mechanic. Though he enjoyed riding, it was the bikes themselves that brought him real joy. Jerry liked their nuts and bolts, to fix them, jury rigging them into things they normally wouldn't be capable of, and just to understand what made them go while seeing them in action.

The sun was gone, night fallen. Crackling, the flames of the small fire they sat around danced. Jerry watched them, sloshing about the beer inside the can he held. Caleb was scowling while Sym grinned like an idiot.

"Something wrong with yours, Jerry?" Caleb's voice was harsh and cold.

"Not that thirsty, I guess," Jerry lied. The ride up the trail was long and dusty. He could use something to drink but beer wasn't it. More than the wrongness in his mind about what they were doing, Jerry worried about the ride back in the dark. Even though they all three pretty much knew the twists, turns, and bumps of the trail by heart, one wrong jerk of a bike or slowed reaction could be a very bad thing.

"Don't be such a pansy," Sym poked at Jerry, stabbing a finger into his side. "This stuff is awesome. I feel like I'm flying!"

And that's exactly what I am worried about, Jerry thought. It was likely the excitement more than the beer itself that had gotten Sym feeling as messed up as he seemed to be, but either way, Jerry didn't want any of it.

"No, really, I'm okay, guys," Jerry assured them.

"You think you're better than us or something?" Caleb stared across the fire with growing anger in his eyes.

"Hey now," Sym turned to Caleb, nearly losing his balance and falling off the stump he sat on. Sym caught himself at the last second. "Whew, that was a close one."

"Stay out of this, Sym," Caleb warned.

"Man, Jerry doesn't think he's better than us," Sym said. "He's just a coward, too afraid to do anything that ain't by the book. Don't you know that?"

Jerry felt a stab of pain at being called a coward. It hurt. He did his best not to let it show. Part of him wondered if Sym was right but regardless, he'd rather be called a coward than get into it with Caleb. The oldest of their trio, Caleb was also the biggest and had scars on his knuckles that showed he wasn't someone you wanted to mess with. Once, they had run into a couple of college punks on the trail, rich boys with shiny, fancy bikes like you'd see at a professional race. The punks made the mistake of thinking they could talk down to Caleb and he had shown them how tough a poor, country boy could be. Caleb almost went to Juvie for breaking one's jaw and the other's arm. It had been a miracle he hadn't. If he got into it himself with Caleb, Jerry figured he would end up on the ground with Caleb stomping in his face.

"Caleb, please," Jerry begged, "I'm just not thirsty. That's all."

"Admit that you're scared," Caleb pressed. "Do that and I'll excuse you being rude by wasting my dad's beer. It wasn't exactly easy to get, ya know."

Like any teenager his age, Jerry didn't want to lose face, not even if it was just in front of Sym. He hesitated a fraction of a second too long in his response and that delay pushed Caleb into a blind rage at his imagined insult.

Caleb jumped up, leaping over the fire between them, to land on Jerry. They crashed to the ground, rolling and struggling. Jerry fought hard not to let Caleb get the upper hand and end up on top of him. He lacked the strength to do it though. Caleb was towering over him, astride his body, when they came to a stop. Jerry was thankful his glasses had gone flying when Caleb tackled him. If they hadn't, they would have broken with his nose as Caleb's fist smashed into it.

"Stop it!" Sym shouted, stumbling over in an attempt to pull Caleb off. Grabbing Caleb by his shoulders, he heaved backwards. It was enough when combined with Jerry's own efforts to get him away. Jerry rolled sideways to put some distance between himself and Caleb.

"Come on, man!" Sym pleaded with Caleb. "He didn't mean nothing and you know it!"

The fight was interrupted as something, massive and inhumanly tall, came crashing out from the trees. With an inhuman roar, one of its huge, hairy hands punched straight through Sym's back, its blood-slicked fist emerging from his chest.

"Holy!" Caleb screamed, scrambling to get out of the thing's path.

At first Jerry thought the creature was a bear. They sometimes moved on two legs. This thing though, it was shaped like a heavily muscled man with overly long arms and clawed hands.

Blood ran from Jerry's nostril. Wiping at it with the backside of his hand, he turned to search the ground for his glasses. Jerry knew he was in shock. He'd just watched Sym die. For the moment, the beast's attention was focused on Caleb. By the fire was Caleb's machete. He always brought it with them whenever they were out riding. Caleb snatched it up, blade gleaming in the dim light of the stars and moon.

"Come on, you bastard!" Caleb wailed. "Let's see how you do against someone who's ready for you!"

Jerry didn't know if Caleb was that drunk or that crazy but either way, what he was doing was utterly irrational. The beast charged him. Jerry didn't stick around to see what happened. He knew there wasn't a chance in Hell that Caleb was going to live through the next few seconds. Jerry poured everything he had into a full out sprint, legs pumping under him. If he could just reach their bikes, maybe, just maybe, he could make it out of the woods alive.

As Jerry ran, Caleb slashed at the huge creature with his machete. As sharp as its blade was, it still didn't cut deeply. The beast's muscles were that dense. It slapped the weapon from Caleb's hand, breaking his wrist in the process. Caleb howled in pain, clutching the arm below his injury with his other hand. The beast moved in even closer, its claws slicing across Caleb's throat, opening it wide in several places. Blood exploded everywhere, into the air, splashing onto the thick hair that covered the beast from head to toe.

Reaching the trail where the bikes were, Jerry didn't look back despite the sound of Caleb's sickening wail being cut short. He kept his focus on the bikes, running to his, and hopping onto it. Jerry fired up its engine and tore along the trail like a bat out of hell.

His mind was reeling from the insanity of it all. His friends were dead, killed by some. . some. . .creature. Jerry knew it had to be a Bigfoot. There was no other logical explanation of what it could be. Still, that was too crazy to accept. Monsters weren't real, were they?

The bike's engine revved, straining to its limits. The trail was dark and the sole headlight only allowed Jerry to see so far ahead of him. He was risking one hell of an accident but didn't give a damn. He had to get away, get help.

Jerry glanced over his shoulder to see the huge monster chasing after him. He was already doing close to forty miles per hour yet somehow the Bigfoot was gaining ground. How in the hell could something so massive move so fast?

Knowing that if he just keep going on along the trail, the Bigfoot would catch up to him, Jerry swerved to the right, down the hill there. The bike bounced, nearly throwing him off but

Jerry held on and managed not to lose control of it. The Bigfoot bounded from the trail, leaping through the air, to land running.

"Damn it!" Jerry yelled. He leaned forward against the bike's handlebars as if trying to make it go faster by just shifting his position. He was approaching the tree line and knew heading into the woods was certain death. Swerving to bring the bike around, he shot by the monster. It lashed out with a clawed hand, slashing through the air near his face. Jerry winced as he felt the claws in his mind even though they had missed him. The creature roared in anger and set out after him again.

Jerry drove parallel to the trail. His head jerked around to see how close the Bigfoot was now only to see that it had closed to being within reach of its long arms. He didn't even have time to scream as a huge, hairy hand closed on his shirt. The Bigfoot yanked him from the bike. It shot onward, front wheel striking a larger rock, and then went flipping end over end with the sound of crunching metal each time it bounced against the ground.

Jerry was flung through the air from where he had been ripped from the bike. He landed hard on his right shoulder, skidding to a stop, several yards from where the Bigfoot had stopped.

Scrambling to his feet, Jerry couldn't use his injured arm at all. It hung limply at his side and hurt like hell. The Bigfoot stood staring at him with burning eyes full of hunger and primal rage. Jerry looked around, desperately, for something, anything that he could use as a weapon against the monster.

The Bigfoot threw its head back in a mighty roar and then charged at him. Jerry tried to stagger out of the monster's path but couldn't manage it. He was struck by nearly a half ton of angry muscle. It was like being hit by a runaway eighteen wheeler. He died instantly. His ribs popped and cracked, folding inward, shards of them piercing his lungs. Blood sprayed from his mouth like vomit from the impact.

The sasquatch howled in the night before settling in to make a meal of those it had killed.

****

Derrick sat, shaking his head, whimpering, "I can't believe she's gone."

Becca, the on-duty dispatcher, had her hands on his shoulders trying to comfort him.

Sheriff Clark handed the deputy a fresh cup of coffee. "Here."

Cradling the cup in his hands, Derrick took a careful sip from it.

After arriving at the campground, Sheriff Clark had put an end to the idea of mounting a search for Manford right then. It had taken some talking but he was able to make Agent Burke and his people see that doing so would only have given Manford the advantage and put them all at farther risk. If they hadn't have found the serial killer's Yukon things might have gone down differently. Without it though, Manford would be forced to flee on foot with no place to go but deeper into the woods. Leaving everyone there except Agent Seymour and Derrick, with additional state troopers called in to support them, he and Agent Burke returned to the station to lay out a proper plan on how to search for Manford.

Sheriff Clark was pretty shaken up by Hannah's death too but not as badly as Derrick. Most of the department knew that there were sparks between them. Agent Seymour seemed disturbed as well. He was sure that she had seen a lot of death, up close and personal before. Still, finding Hannah in such a state, had rattled her too.

Having done what he could for Derrick, Sheriff Clark left him with Becca and Agent Seymour. Agent Burke was waiting in his office, pacing back and forth. He went in, closing the door behind him so that the two of them could talk alone.

"You got a lot of damn nerve showing up in my town and taking over things here, Burke," Sheriff Clark marched around his desk to plop into the chair waiting for him there.

Agent Burke stopped his pacing and spun around to face the sheriff. "I have every right. . ."

"I didn't fragging say you didn't!" Sheriff Clark snapped back. "I am well aware of how things work in cases like this, Burke! I'm just saying if we'd both handled things a bit better maybe one of my deputies wouldn't be dead right now."

Agent Burke huffed, clearly still fuming inside, but bitterly admitted, "Maybe."

"Look, you need me and my people, Burke. We know this town, its people, and the woods surrounding it. I want this bastard as much as you do. I can promise you that. Manford's made this personal. Hannah was a good woman and she's going to be missed a lot around here."

"So what exactly is your plan, Sheriff?" Agent Burke asked.

"At the crack of dawn, we go into those woods, in groups and armed to the teeth. Manford's got no way out of them with all the manpower we left watching the roads and trails out there," Sheriff Clark explained. "And, I'll make some calls before then. By the time the sun is up, we'll have the best tracking dogs in the county with us when we go in. That bastard won't be able to hide from them. I can promise you that."

Sheriff Clark opened the drawer of his desk to get out a map of the area they would be heading into. As he was about to roll it out so they could look at it, Becca came banging on the door to his office.

"Sheriff!" she shouted, knocking furiously again.

Agent Burke, closer to the door, stepped over to let her in.

"I know it's been a hard night for us all, Becca, but you wanna tell me just what in the hell has you so riled up?" Sheriff Clark frowned.

"Deputy Clay just called in," Becca answered.

"Clay?" He interrupted her, knowing that Clay was on the other side of town from where they had Manford hopefully cornered in the mountains.

"Yes sir, Clay was on patrol up near the old Buchanan trail and heard something that sounded like a bad bike wreck. He went to check it out and found three kids dead up there. He said something had torn them apart and ate on them. Said it look like an animal attack."

Agent Burke cocked an eyebrow at Sheriff Clark, giving him a questioning look.

"That ain't all either," Becca went on. "Clay says one of the kids made it to his bike and tried to get away. Didn't do him no good though. From the looks of things, whatever killed him chased him down on it."

"Thank you for letting us know, Becca," Sheriff Clark told her gently. "Why don't you go on home for the night and get some rest. I'm sure we can find someone to take over dispatch for a bit."

She shook her head adamantly. "That wouldn't be right. I got a job to do and I'm gonna do it."

With that, Becca marched out of the office.

Agent Burke shut the door in her wake.

"Is this Old Buchanan Trail on that map of yours?" Agent Burke asked.

"Sure isn't," Sheriff Clark said. "It's on the other side of town from where we saw Manford."

"How the hell did he get through our people, Sheriff? I thought you said we had him."

"He couldn't," Sheriff Clark said.

Agent Burke stared at him waiting on an explanation.

A moment of silence passed before either of them said anything more.

It was Agent Burke who broke it.

"Don't tell me you think Manford isn't working alone anymore," Agent Burke said, "because if you are, let me tell you right now, you're wrong. I know Manford, Sheriff. The man's a loner to his core. He doesn't see anyone else as more than a tool to be used or a victim to slash open."

"Maybe he's changed," Sheriff Clark sighed. "'Cause there isn't any way in hell he could have made it over there to kill those kids that fast even if he had a car and our people weren't blocking the roads and trails surrounding the campground. It's impossible given the timing and distance."

Agent Burke plopped into the chair in front of Sheriff Clark's desk and steepled his fingers together over his lips. "You're sure?"

"Positive," Sheriff Clark nodded.

****

Deputy Daryl sat on the hood of the patrol car, puffing away on a cigarette. The driver's door was open where Frank, the lead deputy, reclined watching the trees.

"Ain't none of this right," Deputy Daryl said. "People don't get murdered around these parts and now, how many have been tonight? I've lost count, haven't you? Five?"

"Eight," Frank corrected the younger deputy.

Daryl whistled and repeated the word, "Eight! That's really messed up."

"Well, what do you think happens when a serial killer the FBI seem to be falling over themselves to catch comes to town?"

"It's like that Carpenter movie, the old one with the guy dressed in black wearing a Captain Kirk mask," Daryl flung his cigarette onto the gravel road and leaped from the car's hood to grind what was left of it out with the heel of his boot.

"I swear," Daryl turned his head to grin at Frank. "The sheriff needs to give us a pay raise after tonight."

Frank chuckled. "You keep telling yourself that, Daryl."

"You really think that sicko freak is still out there in these woods?" Daryl rapped his knuckles on the side of the patrol car.

Frank sighed and got up from where he sat. Reaching back into the car, he picked up the shotgun that lay resting in the passenger seat before closing the driver's door.

"Ain't no way out for that bastard," Frank swore. "He's ours. It's only a matter of time."

Daryl shook his head. "Wish I had your faith in that, Frank. You ain't never seen First Blood have you? Rambo came to town and tore that entire sheriff department apart. Did any of them live? Nah, I don't think so."

"That bastard out there. . ." Frank said, keeping his voice calm, "Manford isn't a green beret. He's just some freak that gets his kicks from dressing up like a monster and killing people."

"Gotta be damn smart," Daryl argued. "The FBI ain't caught him yet, have they?"

Frank grunted and Daryl changed the subject.

"When I was a kid my old man used to bring me hunting up here," Daryl commented. "He was a third generation bear hunter. We shot some real big ones back then too. Loved every minute of it. These days. . ." Daryl shrugged, his expression suddenly saddened, "I reckon these woods have been hunted out. The bears just ain't around like they used to be. Really have to put some effort into finding one now."

Daryl kept rambling on about the dogs he and his father had used for their hunting and his memories of them but Frank had quit listening.

His attention was focused on the trees across from where the patrol car was parked in the middle of the road, its lights in cruise mode. Something had set off his nerves. He couldn't see a damn thing out there in the shadows but it sure as hell felt like they were being watched all of a sudden.

"Daryl," Frank snapped.

The younger deputy's words stuttered to an abrupt halt and his hand went to the butt of the pistol holstered on his belt. The tone of Frank's voice tipping him off that something was up.

"What is it?" Daryl asked in a quiet, hushed voice.

"I don't know yet," Frank kept his eyes fixed on the trees. "Could be nothin'."

"Nah," Daryl shook his head. "It ain't nothing. Trouble's come calling."

Neither of them saw the seven foot tall, hairy creature charge from the trees behind the patrol car, sprinting towards them, until it was halfway across the road.

"Holy mother!" Daryl yelped at the sight of it.

Frank's shotgun swung up into a firing position but with the car between them and the creature, he didn't have a clear shot at the thing. Its black lips were parted in a feral snarl, eyes glowing red with a fierceness that chilled Frank to his bones on a primal level. All he wanted to do was throw his shotgun down and run like hell. Frank stood his ground though.

The creature's feet left the road in a jump that carried on top of the patrol car. The lights there shattered and the roof collapsed inward from the weight that landed on it. The windows blew out from the sudden pressure on them. Shards of broken glass sprayed over him as Frank twisted his upper body away from the direction of the car. A shard left a trail of red where it grazed his cheek and another imbedded itself in the backside of his right hand. Daryl was cursing like a sailor, his forehead smeared with blood that the younger deputy was hurriedly attempting to clear from his eyes. Then the creature on top of the car hopped down to land next to him.

Frank had never seen anything like the thing in his entire life. It wore no clothes but had the overall shape of a man. Its arms were a touch too long and blazing eyes utterly inhuman. The teeth in its mouth were jagged and pointed. He watched in shock and sheer terror as the creature lifted Daryl up over its head, as if the young deputy weighed nothing at all, and ripped him in half. Daryl's entrails spilled out over the creature as it was drenched by his blood.

"Hellfire!" Frank exclaimed, swinging his shotgun to level its barrel at the creature. He didn't know if the thing was a werewolf or what in the hell it was but surely a twelve gauge slug would knock the thing on its ass, if nothing else.

He squeezed the shotgun's trigger. It thundered, bucking in his hands. The creature was struck, dead on, in the center of its chest by the heavy slug. Frank worked the shotgun's pump, chambering another round and firing again even as the creature staggered backwards. The second round that slammed into its chest was enough to take the thing down. It fell onto the road, loosing a high pitched shriek that reminded Frank of a wounded cat. He pumped a third round into the chamber of the shotgun and kept the weapon aimed at the thing where it lay on the road. The whatever the hell is was clearly wasn't dead. Pushing its body partially erect with its hands, the thing was trying to get up.

"Frag me," Frank muttered, watching it. The thing's chest was a mass of torn up muscle and freely flowing blood and yet there was fight still in its eyes as they locked on him. Raising his shotgun higher, Frank took aim at the creature's face and squeezed the trigger. It caved inward as the heavy slug he fired punched through flesh and bone to exit out the other side of the thing's head. The creature thudded onto the road, this time still and unmoving. A puddle of red spread outward around its skull.

Frank collapsed to his knees, sucking in one ragged breath after another. His heart was pounding, booming in his ears. Frank knew he needed to calm himself down before he had a heart attack. Seeing the creature wasn't going to be getting up again, Frank closed his eyes and fought to steady his breathing. After a few seconds ticked by, it had leveled out. With a strained grunt, the lead deputy heaved himself up. Glancing over at the two pieces of Daryl and the red-slicked, purple strands of intestines spilling out of them, Frank swallowed hard, resisting the urge to throw up. He staggered over to the patrol car, trying to get to its radio. The doors were wedged shut somehow by its collapsed roof. He leaned against the side of the car and dug around in the pocket of his pants to produce his cell. He found Sheriff Clark's personal number in contacts and stabbed the screen of his phone with his thumb to dial it.

****

Less than twenty minutes later, Sheriff Clark and Agent Burke were on scene. An ambulance had arrived too and its paramedics were busy collecting Deputy Daryl's corpse to be taken to the coroner's office. After taking a moment to warn the paramedics to keep their mouths shut about what they had seen, Sheriff Clark joined Frank where the still somewhat in shock lead deputy stood watching Agent Burke examine the dead creature's hair-covered body.

"That thing just came out of nowhere," Frank stammered. "Daryl was dead before either of us could do anything."

"It's not your fault, Frank," Sheriff Clark placed a reassuring hand on the lead deputy's shoulder.

"I don't think his mother's going to see it that way, Sheriff," Frank's voice was thick with emotion.

"Sheriff!" Agent Burke called out, motioning for him to come over and join him.

Agent Burke finished poking at the monster's dead body with the pen he held and got up. "Any idea what this thing is?"

"I was hoping you could tell me," Sheriff Clark admitted. "I ain't never seen anything like it."

"Me either," Agent Burke frowned. "You think this thing is our other killer?"

Sheriff Clark sighed and shook his head. "I

don't see how this thing would have gotten across town without being noticed, much less in the right time frame to have killed those kids and be back here already."

"We don't know anything about it," Agent Burke protested. "For all we know, this thing can fly."

"You really believe that?" Sheriff Clark smirked.

"Ha. No. I was merely making a point," Agent Burke chuckled. "I think you're right though, be it for a different reason. We have samples of tracks left by Manford's Bigfoot suit. They're actually larger than this thing's feet, only slightly, but still larger."

"Is that what this thing is?" Sheriff Clark asked.

"From the looks of it, I'd think not. It's too small," Agent Burke seemed to hesitate as if not wanting to go on.

"There's a but coming, ain't there?" Sheriff Clark stared at the FBI agent.

Agent Burke nodded. "What if this thing," he kicked the creature's body, "is just a kid?"

Sheriff Clark shuddered. "That would mean. . ."

"That its parents are out there somewhere," Agent Burke frowned.

"Damn," Sheriff Clark gritted his teeth. "I think we're in trouble, Burke."

"You and me both, Sheriff," Agent Burke fished a piece of gum from his pocket and shoved it into his mouth. "But if this thing does have a father, mother, or both out there in these woods it sure as hell explains everything, doesn't it?"

"We're gonna have to assume that it does. Not doing that and being wrong could get a lot more of our people killed," Sheriff Clark eyed the trees. The night somehow seemed to have grown much darker around them.

"And based on this thing here, we're also going to need some bigger guns," Agent Burke said.

****

As the sun rose over Green Grove Campground, the place was filled with state troopers, federal agents, paramedics, and most of Sheriff Clark's department. There were a few journalists too but they didn't seem to really understand the full reality of what was going on. Sheriff Clark and, even more so, Agent Burke was glad of that.

Agent Burke was watching the chaos with a grim expression.

"You wishing we'd decided to give the national guard a call?" Sheriff Clark half joked.

"Come on," Agent Burke ignored the sheriff's playful jab. "Let's get this show started."

The tracking dogs that Sheriff Clark had called in sat around their owners waiting for a scent to be given to them. Agents Owens and Seymour, along with a few volunteers from Burke's forensics crew, mingled with the local deputies. It was them that would be going into the woods with the dogs and their handlers. There were no state troopers in the group. All of them were busy holding the line around the woods and campground as well as keeping the journalists out.

"Okay, people!" Agent Burke bellowed, almost shouting so that everyone could hear. "All of you are to stick to the sections of the search grid you've been assigned to. I want all of you to stay alert out there. Manford, by himself, is one cunning, cold blooded bastard, and dangerous enough. As you know however, we very well may be dealing with other threats in those woods too."

Agent Burke knew that Sheriff Clark had shown all of his deputies the body of the creature that his lead deputy managed to kill before having it loaded into the rear of a hearse, the only thing easily at hand that could handle it. The corpse of the creature was too large to deal with easily in an ambulance. He'd done the same for Agents Owens and Seymour. Allowing their people to see the creature with their own eyes was what had to be done in order to ensure they would believe something like it actually existed. All of them had been sworn to secrecy too until told otherwise by himself or the sheriff. That in itself would have been more of a risk were not everyone who saw the beast headed straight into the woods as part of the manhunt, not giving any of them a chance to talk to the press or anyone else.

Agent Seymour was paired with Deputy Derrick. Agent Owens with Clay. The lead deputy, Frank, who had killed the creature, was paired with a forensics agent named Steven who had little experience in hunts like this. Agent Burke would be heading into the woods with the sheriff at his side. Each pair was accompanied by its own group of dogs and handler too. They were all local and handpicked by the sheriff who swore that they would get the job of locating Manford done.

"If you encounter Manford, or anything else of concern out there, radio it in. I don't want any heroics or stupid, overconfident mistakes out there," Agent Burke barked. "Do I make myself clear, folks?"

Everyone nodded.

"Alright then," Agent Burke concluded his speech. "Let's be about it then!"

The dogs were given Manford's scent from an old piece from one of the serial killer's old beast suits that Agent Burke had on hand, then the searchers entered the woods with the early sun high above them.

Bethany was the name of the handler that was with Agent Burke and the sheriff. Agent Seymour and Derrick's dog handler was a redneck dude by the name of Earl. Agent Owens and Clay were with a butch lady named Trudi. And Frank and Steven's was Gary, a long bearded, older man.

The handlers all kept a tight reign on their dogs, who barked loudly and strained on their leashes as the hunt began. The dogs were all headed in the same direction at first but quickly seemed to become confused. Their eagerness to charge on ahead lessened. Some of the dogs even whined and tucked their tails between their legs. The groups broke off in different directions, some of the dogs going ahead without needing to be chided along, others not. Regardless all of them were u

****

Agent Seymour and Derrick veered farthest to the northwest. Their dogs didn't act like they had any sort of sense of Manford's trail. Instead, they were rather passive and simply being led along rather than leading the group. Derrick could tell the day was going to be a hot one for the season. Already sweat was beading on his forehead. He wiped it away and shook his head.

"You okay there, Derrick?" Earl snickered.

Glaring at him, the deputy frowned. "I'm fine, Earl."

"Don't look it," Earl commented. "Gonna be a long day out here."

"Your dogs don't appear to be doing too well either," Agent Seymour pointed out.

Earl snorted.

"She's right, Earl. What in the devil is going on with them?" Derrick asked. He had worked with Earl and the dogs before and knew for sure that something was up. They weren't acting right at all.

Agent Seymour was aware of Derrick's encounter with Manford before the search and was glad to see the pale deputy responding to their situation instead of getting lost in his obvious fears and grief. She'd been worried about having him along with her. Not many could live through what he had and see what he'd seen without being royally screwed up by it. Manford might not be one of the beasts that it was becoming clear were out there somewhere but his suit could be just as horrifying. That deputy hadn't spent the time chasing the serial killer that she had. Still, it wasn't to say that the deputy was truly okay. She was sure Derrick would be haunted by his encounter with Manford and the slashed up wreck of a face of his fellow deputy, Hannah, for the rest of his life and never forget it. Agent Seymour could easily imagine him waking up screaming from nightmares of the beast. The sound of the dog handler's reply pulled her own focus back to where it needed to be.

"They're spooked," Earl admitted. "Ain't never seen them like this."

"If you need to take them back. . ." Agent Seymour offered.

"My boys will get this job done," Earl assured her, "I can promise you that."

As the day wore on, trudging through the woods got more difficult and even Earl was sweating. There were several upward inclines up the hills that the woods led towards and continued on beyond. The dogs never got better. If anything, the mood of the dogs got worse.

The trio came to a stop as the dogs refused to go any further. Earl knelt, rubbing them and encouraging them. They were outright whimpering now.

"What the hell is wrong with them?" Agent Seymour demanded.

"Like I said, they're spooked, lady," Earl explained. "Something out here has got them scared out of their heads."

"You should've just admitted they weren't up to this," Agent Seymour chided the big handler.

"Lady," Earl stood up, towering over the FBI agent, "I got enough trouble without you telling me about how right you think you were."

Agent Seymour stood her ground, not intimidated by him in the slightest. Earl grunted and went back over to his dogs.

Derrick moved to her side and whispered, "He doesn't know about the creature. The handlers weren't shown that thing's body."

Agent Seymour's eyes went wide.

"I thought. . ." she stammered.

"Nope. Just us deputies and your agents that were actually going into the woods," Derrick said. "I'm getting the feeling all of us should turn back. We haven't seen any sign of Manford anyway."

"You know, even seeing that thing, I. . I can't

quite make myself believe creatures like it exist."

"Oh, trust me, I know what you mean," Derrick nodded. "I'm man enough to admit the look of that thing scares the hell out of me."

"What y'all whispering about over there?" Earl glared at them. From his expression Derrick figured the big man thought they were talking crap about his dogs.

"Nothing that concerns you," Agent Seymour answered before Derrick could.

"That so?" Earl puffed out his chest, cheeks red, pride apparently hurting.

"Really, Earl," Derrick said. "We're talking about the killer out here and some things we're not allowed to discuss about him. That's all."

Earl didn't look to believe him.

"We have an idea of what's going on with your dogs and it's not their fault," Agent Seymour said and Derrick wished she hadn't.

"Yeah?" Earl eyed her. "What do you think is out here?"

"Weren't you listening, Earl?" Derrick tried to be as gentle as he could with the big handler's feelings. "We can't tell you."

"That's messed up," Earl's expression remained angry and mistrustful. "I can't help my boys get back on track to catch that killer of yours if you're keeping things I need to know from me."

"Not our choice," Agent Seymour frowned.

"There's a lot of sun left in the day," Earl's head flicked upwards at the sky. "We gonna just stand around here wasting it?"

Derrick didn't remind the big handler that it was his dogs that they had stopped for. "No," he answered and then glanced at Agent Seymour. "We doing this or heading in?"

"Let's keep going." Agent Seymour walked on the way they had been going. It was obvious to Derrick that she didn't really want to though.

Earl's dogs went nuts, desperately fighting to break loose and get away. The big man struggled to reign them in but couldn't. The dogs tore free and disappeared into the trees, running like hell back towards the campground. That was the only warning they got. None of them had time to react as the hulking mass of muscle, hair, and primal rage emerged from the trees. It backhanded Agent Seymour as it crashed past her, charging at Earl. Her jaw shattered, teeth and blood flying. Knocked from her feet, Agent Seymour went rolling across the grass. Earl could only stare at the monster in shock and disbelief. Derrick managed not to freeze up but still couldn't get his shotgun up in time to have a shot at the thing before it reached the big handler. Earl died as huge hands clutched his head and ripped it away from his shoulders in an explosion of red.

"No!" Derrick heard himself yell.

Agent Seymour was down, body twitching. There would be no help coming from her. Derrick saw that he was on his own and if he didn't stop the monster, it would kill him too. Hands trembling, centering the barrel of his shotgun level with the monster's chest, Derrick squeezed the trigger. The shotgun boomed. The blast caught the beast full on at its sternum. It stumbled a few steps but quickly regained its footing, black lips parting in a furious snarl.

"God help me," Derrick muttered, wondering how in the hell that thing was still standing. His eyes told Derrick that his shot hadn't gotten any real penetration through the monster's thick muscles but that was impossible, wasn't it?Working the shotgun's pump to chamber another round, Derrick locked eyes with the beast. It was like looking into the depths of hell. The beast launched itself at him with such speed, Derrick wasn't able to get off a second shot. He was forced to leap sideways, dodging the huge monster's mad charge. He spun, firing at its back as it passed him by. It missed the monstrous beast, striking a nearby tree. Splinters of wood exploded from its trunk.

The beast came about, turning to face him. Derrick was ready for it to rush him again, his shotgun braced against his shoulder. Instead, it dashed away into the woods. Cursing, Derrick lowered his weapon, not willing to waste another round.

He lost sight of the beast as it ran. Somehow, the thing melted into the woods, perfectly blending with them. Derrick's breaths came in ragged gasps. He was just short of hyperventilating, heart fluttering in his chest. The cracking and snapping of tree limbs and rustling of bushes stopped somewhere to his right. Derrick whirled, gaze scanning the woods for any sign of the great beast. If the beast was there, Derrick couldn't see it.

A pained moan arose from Agent Seymour. She'd stopped twitching and just lay on the grass bleeding. Derrick was a little surprised that she was alive. Her face was so smashed up from the single blow it took from the beast that it looked like some sort of insane piece of abstract art. Derrick wanted to go to her but was rooted to the spot where he stood. He didn't dare move, at least not until it was clear that the beast was gone or dead. There were only three rounds remaining in his shotgun and Derrick very much doubted that they would be enough to stop the beast. A direct shot to its chest sure as hell hadn't done much.

Did the beast know he was waiting on it? Was it that intelligent? Derrick didn't know much about Sasquatch, if in fact that was what the creature was. Everything pointed to that. What else could it be? Derrick swallowed, his mouth dry, and kept his gaze fixed on the trees. On the upside, his hands had finally stopped trembling.

Derrick braced the shotgun against his shoulder, sweeping its barrel side to side along the length of the woods in front of him. Something came flying from out of them. It wasn't the beast. A broken tree limb spun end over end through the air, striking Derrick with enough force to knock his shotgun from his hands and send him toppling over backwards. He was screaming as the beast burst out in its wake. Derrick scrambled to get to his feet and draw the pistol holstered on his hip. The beast was on him though before he could do either. One of its huge feet caught him in the chest, pressing him down onto his back. Sickening snapping and popping noises could be heard as his ribs gave way beneath the beast's weight.

Derrick died instantly.

****

The group of Agent Owens, Clay, and their dog handler Trudi were the closest to where Derrick's group had met its end. Hearing the shotgun blasts in the distance, they came to an abrupt halt.

"What the hell was that?" Agent Owens asked.

"Shotgun blast," Clay answered. "More than one."

"Let's go," Agent Owens ordered, calling it in as the group ran in the direction the blasts came from.

"This is Agent Owens!" she cried over her radio. "We've got gun shots fired to our east from Agent Seymour's section of the search grid!"

None of them were expecting what happened next. A massive beast, far too large and furious to be a man in a Bigfoot suit, met Agent Owens head on. Overly large, hair-covered hands snatched the agent up from the ground and flung her into a nearby tree. Agent Owens' body bent around it, the impact breaking her spine. Her corpse bounced from the rough trunk to land crumpled in the grass.

"Holy!" Clay wailed, skidding to a stop and beginning to backpedal away from the huge beast. Trudi's dog broke loose, darting off into the woods, yelping as they went.

"No! Come back!" Trudi shouted at her dogs but they weren't listening.

Clay was carrying an AR-15 converted to full auto. He opened up on the beast with it. The bullets left small patches of red where they struck the beast but didn't get any real penetration. All they seemed to do was make the creature angrier than it already was.

Trudi was armed with a .357 Magnum and yanked the heavy revolver from its holster. Cocking its hammer with her thumb, she aimed the weapon at the beast. The revolver boomed as she fired a round that thudded into the beast's shoulder. The shot did far more damage than Clay's AR had been able to inflict. The pain from the wound caused the beast to spring forward, passing Clay in almost a blur. Trudi screamed as huge hands tore both her arms from their sockets. She reeled about, blood pumping from where they'd been attached.

Clay watched in horror as the dog handler stumbled towards him. The beast reached out to grab her again though and plucked Trudi's head from her shoulders. A geyser of blood sprayed upwards from its stump. Her corpse collapsed at its feet and the beast brought her skull to its mouth, taking a loud, crunching bite as if it were an apple. Blood and brain matter oozed from its lips as the beast chewed what it had bitten off.

Screaming a berserker war cry, Clay hosed the beast with fully automatic fire from his AR, finger tight on the trigger until the rest of the weapon's magazine was spent. The beast stood its ground. Though clearly pained, it didn't even so much as stagger, taking all the damage he could throw its way. Then with a roar louder than that of a lion's the beast rushed forward. Clay flipped his AR around, swinging the weapon like a club. Its butt shattered against the muscles of the beast's wounded shoulder. That did stagger it. The beast recoiled, giving Clay the precious seconds needed to draw the Glock holstered on his belt. He knew there was no hope in Hell of the 9mm pistol bringing the beast down unless he targeted his shots well.

The beast, already recovered, sprang at him again. Aiming carefully, Clay put a round into its left eye. The beast's head reared back as the bullet entered, reducing the eyeball to a mess of watery, red pulp inside its socket. Clay fired twice more. He was aiming for the softer flesh of the beast's throat. Its head came down again just in time to prevent that. They struck its chin, tearing through hair and skin to flatten against bone. Their impact stunned the beast. Clay was thrown by the bullets missing their target. It caused him to hesitate. The swipe of a clawed hand broke his right wrist and knocked his Glock out of his grasp. The beast pressed in on him. Clay frantically scrambled to get the hell away from it. Tears born of pain wet his eyes. He could see the white of bone poking out of his broken wrist which was bent sideways at an unnatural angle. His wrist throbbed with each movement he made. If he didn't move though, he would be dead.

Left with no weapon available to him, Clay's only option was to make a run for it. Twisting around he attempted to do just that. The beast was already too close and there was no escaping the reach of its long arms. They closed around Clay. He screamed, lifted from the ground in the beast's embrace. It hugged him tight like a bear, crushing his body to its chest. He couldn't breathe. Squirming, feet thrashing, Clay struggled to break free. He was so desperate that Clay even bit into one of the beast's arms. Hot blood coated his tongue and smeared his lips as he chewed, trying to cause enough pain for the beast to drop him. He spat hair and meat. The beast didn't let go. It squeezed tighter. Clay's body crumpled beneath the pressure of the beast's hold. He died emptying the last of the breath that remained in his burning, oxygen deprived lungs.

****

Manford came to a stop, bracing himself with a single hand stuck out against the trunk of a tree. He'd spent a good portion of the night running and even now kept pushing himself on at the best pace his exhausted body could manage. Sweat slicked his body inside the suit he thought of as his second skin. The night was bad enough. Now that the sun was up, Manford was cooking inside his second skin. His heart seemed on the verge of exploding and his lungs burned. The sun was high in the sky, approaching its zenith for the day.

Glancing about Manford realized that he had no idea where in the hell he was. Fleeing the FBI and the local cops, his flight had taken him deep into the woods, into their hills and valleys. He had eluded the bastards at least though, for the time being. He cursed himself for allowing his bloodlust to override his need to get the hell out of town. He had known how dangerous it was to kill again in the area. The federal agent assigned to bring him in was a real hard nose bastard who didn't give up. Burke, that was his name, and his people kept getting closer and closer. Manford never worried too much about them but today violating his own rules was costing him dearly. Odds were his van was in their hands now. He held little hope that it hadn't been discovered. Manford didn't dare return to where it was parked. Thanks to his own stupid mistake, he was now cut off from his van and the supplies it held, left with nothing but what was on him, and no real idea of which direction to be heading in.

Manford was sure of one thing. His second skin wasn't coming off no matter how uncomfortable it got. He was nude beneath it. That had nothing to do with his reasoning for remaining in it. Out here, this was the home of his people or at least places like this one. This was where the Sasquatch dwelled. Manford tingled with the thrill that he might encounter them. He longed to be with the creatures he considered his family. It was his destiny one day. Perhaps he would find them while out here in such dense and remote woodland. Manford called out to any Sasquatch who might be close enough to hear, intoning a series of grunts and roars. He waited for a reply but only silence answered him. He did hear something though. Inclining his head sideways like the animal he was within his mind, Manford focused on the noise, realizing at last what was making it. His long legged, well muscled body bounded in the direction the noise came from. He plowed straight through lower lying, thin branches, shielding himself with his arms before him like a shield. The trees opened up into a clearing through which a small stream trickled. Manford dropped on his knees next to the water. Carefully, ever so carefully, his hands reached up and removed the head of his second skin and placed it gently in the grass. Leaning forward, Manford drank like the animal he longed to be, lapping at the moving water. He drank for a long time, getting his fill. The water was cool and restored his strength. Finally, he stopped, wiping at the wetness on his chin with the backside of his hand. Manford shook his head wildly like a dog attempting to dry itself and then replaced the head of his second skin, sealing himself inside his Bigfoot suit once more.

Manford rose to his full, towering height. He could feel the static charge about in the air. A storm was coming. . .a very bad one. It was not something he wanted to be caught out in. He needed to find somewhere to hunker down, take shelter until it passed, but where? He had seen no cabins or any sort of dwellings in the woods so far during his mad flight from the agents and cops pursuing him. He intoned a series of savage grunts, crying out to his people once more. Still, there was no answer. He was on his own as he ever was.

A vague memory surfaced in his mind. His knowledge of this area was extremely limited but somewhere Manford believed that he had heard there were caves up in the hills of this area. He doubted they would be easy to find but they were his only hope. Manford set out at a steady pace northward.

In the sky above, dark clouds gathered like an army amassing to loose their fury upon the world below. Half an hour later, rain began to fall as flashes of lightning danced about the sky and thunder rolled. Manford's luck held and he came upon a cave in the side of a hill while the storm was in its infant stages. Without any worry of what might be lurking inside, Manford hurried into the cave. It was dark and dank but empty. The cave only extended a few dozen yards into the hillside, nowhere near as large or deep as Manford had expected it to be. As a wave of thunder crashed outside, he settled into a comfortable spot amid the cave's shadows and watched the storm outside close in.

****

Bethany's dogs suddenly went crazy, yipping and barking. They had picked up Manford's scent. Agent Burke and Sheriff Clark hurried along with her and the dogs. Sheriff Clark worked the pump of the shotgun he carried, readying the weapon. He was glad to see that Agent Burke wasn't screwing around. The FBI agent had brought a Uzi into the woods with him. Sheriff Clark hoped the little submachine gun was as lethal as it looked if they were the first ones to stumble onto Manford. So far as they knew, the sick bastard had managed to give them all the slip. There sure as hell hadn't been any sign of him yet. Not a single group of their search parties had radioed in anything since Agent Owens had reported hearing shots from Agent Seymour's section of the grid. That news had brought all of the groups running. The woods were large though and even the locals and dog handlers faced difficulty navigating it in the rain that had begun to fall in waves. It had been light at first but quickly grown into a downpour that limited their visibility and darkened the woods around them.

Sheriff Clark thought it odd that neither

Agent Seymour or Agent Owens' groups were responding over the radio. As good as Manford supposedly was, not even someone like him could stand up to that many armed and trained people. He hoped that it was just something with the storm that was messing with their communications. If it wasn't. . .well, he didn't want to think about that because it would mean their people had run into something else entirely.

Bethany brought the dogs to a halt. Agent Burke and Sheriff Clark stopped behind her. The dogs were straining at their leashes and yapping but Bethany shushed them.

"What is it?" Agent Burke asked.

"I think we've got your man," Bethany grinned. Her long, red hair was soaked and plastered to her head by the rain. She was pale skinned and thin with long legs. Agent Burke had a difficult time meeting her green eyes. They stirred feelings that he thought were long dead and didn't care for that.

Bethany gestured at something through the pouring rain. Agent Burke squinted in the direction she indicated, trying to see what she did. Sheriff Clark saw it first.

"There's a cave in the side of that hill," Sheriff Clark said.

Agent Burke finally saw what they had. It was indeed the mouth of a cave, small, dark and almost completely obscured by the rain, trees, and overgrowth surrounding its entrance.

"We can't be this lucky," Agent Burke huffed.

"Sure looks like we are," Sheriff Clark chuckled.

"Should I let my dogs loose?" Bethany asked. Agent Burke could see that the animals weren't just track dogs but likely trained killers too. There were regulations to think about so he shook his head.

"No," Agent Burke told her. "We'll go in there ourselves."

"We will?" Sheriff Clark balked.

"What were you thinking of doing then?" Agent Burke challenged him. "Just waiting around out here in the rain until Manford shows himself?"

Sheriff Clark grunted but didn't say anything more.

"Bethany, I want you to stay here," Agent Burke ordered, "I mean right here. I don't want you going near that cave. If we don't come out, radio for help."

"And if Manford comes out instead of you guys?" Bethany frowned.

"Run like hell and don't look back," Sheriff Clark told her.

"You got it," Bethany nodded.

"How about it?" Agent Burke asked. "You ready for this?"

"As I ever will be," Sheriff Clark huffed.

The two of them crept towards the mouth of the cave, leaving Bethany and her dogs behind. She had gotten the dogs calm and they sat silently now awaiting a new command from her.

Agent Burke was in the lead, approaching the cave mouth from its left side through the rain. Sheriff Clark came in from the right. They met at the edges of the mouth, looking across its darkness at one another. Both had their weapons at the ready. The interior of the cave was silent and still but if the dogs had steered them right, it certainly wasn't empty.

Sheriff Clark pointed at the muddy ground. Agent Burke looked down to see the tracks there. They were identical, as best as he could tell, to those that belonged to Manford's whacko suit that the serial killer wore when he took the lives of his victims. Agent Burke noticed something else too. The tracks led into. . .and out of the cave. He opened his mouth to warn Sheriff Clark but it was too late. Manford leaped out from the bushes behind where the sheriff stood. The razor blades that served as Manford's claws left trails of red in their wake, slashing down Sheriff Clark's back. The sheriff swung around to confront the serial killer only to have the claws of Manford's other hand slice open the soft flesh of his throat. Sheriff Clark's shotgun fell from his hands as they reached up, trying to stem the blood that pumped rapidly from the mess the claw-like blades had left in their wake. Eyes wide, he glanced over at Agent Burke one final time and then died. Sheriff Clark's body thudded onto the ground.

Manford was gone having ducked back into the trees he had emerged from. Agent Burke held his fire. He even managed not to scream as he stood watching the puddle of rain water surrounding Sheriff Clark's body turning red. Positioning himself to where his back touched the rock of the hill next to the cave's mouth, Agent Burke's eyes scanned the trees. Manford was out there somewhere and would strike again as soon as he saw the chance to do so. . . unless. . .unless he went after Bethany instead. If he held his position, Bethany would be out there alone with no idea that Manford might be coming for her next. If he moved to warn Bethany and join up with her, doing so would leave him exposed with no one watching his back as he ran through the woods to reach her.

"Screw it!" Agent Burke flung himself away from the hillside and sprinted into the trees. His legs pumped beneath him and his breath came in ragged gasps as he ran for where Bethany was supposed to be waiting for them to return.

Agent Burke had waited so long for this confrontation with Manford, wanted it so badly, but this was nothing like he had imagined. This was all wrong. The woods were giving Manford an advantage that he wasn't quite sure how to counter. He was well aware of the suit the serial killer designed and created for himself. Still, Agent Burke would have never believed the thing would actually work as real world camo. The suit though was doing just that and uncannily so.

Bethany and her dogs saw him coming. The dogs began to bark and growl, readying themselves to protect their master.

"Look out!" Agent Burke yelled. "Manford could be anywhere!"

Before she could ask, he added, "The sheriff's dead. Manford got him right out the cave."

"God protect us," Bethany crossed herself. Unlike most of the other handlers, she wasn't carrying a gun. Agent Burke yanked his pistol from its holster and tossed it at her. Bethany caught the weapon, though her expression was one of utter distaste.

"I hate guns," she said though she worked its slide, readying the Glock like a professional.

Agent Burke cocked an eyebrow at her.

"I said I hate them," Bethany frowned, "not that I don't know how to use them."

The two of them stood, side by side, with the dogs milling about around them.

"Let 'em go," Agent Burke told Bethany.

"I can't promise they'll go after Manford," she warned.

"Just do it," he motioned at the dogs.

Bethany released them. The dogs took off into the trees, scattering in different directions as they went. There was no means of knowing if some of them were heading after the serial killer or not.

Seconds ticked by and the sound of the dogs' barking grew more distant.

"We can't just stand here forever, Burke," Bethany said.

He looked around again, still seeing no sign of Manford. There was no denying that Bethany was right. They needed to make a move. The question was did they head back to the campground, try to hook up with another search group, or go on the offensive, actively hunting for Manford?

"This is Burke," he said over his radio. "Manford is in our search grid. Be advised, the suit he's wearing is highly effective as camouflage."

With the others informed of Manford's current location, Agent Burke motioned for Bethany to follow him and started eastward. He clutched his Uzi tightly and hoped that the call he was making was the right one. Frank's party was the closest to their location based on the last radio check in before Manford struck. It was Agent Burke's hope to meet up with them. The old saying that there was safety in numbers was true.

"Where do you think Manford's gone to?" Bethany asked as they walked cautiously amid the trees.

"Hell if I know," Agent Burke snapped without meaning to. The stress was getting to him and it was showing.

Manford swung out from behind the wide trunk of a tree, right on top of them from their left flank. Agent Burke raised his Uzi, using it as a shield as the killer's razor blade claws came slashing in. Metal sparked against metal as he managed to block the attack. Agent Burke lashed out, kicking Manford in the mid-section.

With a grunt, the big killer was staggered. Pressing his attack, Agent Burke swung the extended stock of his Uzi up to catch the underside of Manford's chin. The killer's head snapped backwards atop his neck. Agent Burke followed through, striking again, with another blow that smashed into the side of Manford's head. Agent Burke blinked, shocked the killer was still on his feet and in that moment, things shifted. Though not fully recovered, Manford hurled himself forward anyway, throwing the whole of his weight onto Agent Burke. The FBI man was knocked from his feet, thudding onto the ground with Manford coming down on top of him. Desperately clinging to his Uzi, the weapon ended up between the two of them with both of them grasping it.

Bethany stood with the pistol Agent Burke gave her aimed at Manford. She didn't have a clear shot. Feeling helpless, she watched the two of them struggling for the Uzi. Agent Burke appeared to be winning despite Manford's size. The killer's suit utterly freaked Bethany out. It was like something from a nightmare given life in the real world. The suit truly did give Manford the appearance of being a Sasquatch. Even its teeth looked real.

Agent Burke didn't realize what Manford was

up to until it was too late. The big serial killer was playing him. Manford didn't want the Uzi at all. He just wanted him preoccupied and it worked. Suddenly one of Manford's hands let go of the Uzi and took another swipe at him. Agent Burke screamed as razor blade claws cut deeply over his face. His nose separated across its bridge, blood spurting, as a claw raked across it. He also lost his right eye. A blade divided the eye in two along its length, inside the socket where it rested. The eye's pulpy innards were leaking out of it. The other blades opened the flesh of his forehead and cheek. Agent Burke's head snapped backwards out of reflex, smashing into the ground he lay on. His vision was blinded by blood and pain. He heard Bethany's pistol crack three times in rapid succession. Manford leaped away from him, to his feet. Bethany's pistol fired twice more as the hulking form of the serial killer in his Sasquatch suit dived sideways into the trees.

The next thing Agent Burke knew, Bethany was kneeling over him, her eyes filled with concern and gleaming tears.

"Agent Burke!" she shrieked. "Agent Burke, are you okay?"

He could only do his best to nod.

"I think he's gone," Bethany told him. "I hit

him several times. I know I did."

"You. . .did good," Agent Burke croaked, red bubbling from his split nose accompanied by a sickening almost gargling noise. "Help me up."

She did, straining to get him onto his feet. With one of his arms resting over her shoulders, Bethany supported enough of his weight to allow Agent Burke to stand.

"Get my Uzi," he ordered her. "We're going to need it if Manford comes back."

Bethany helped Agent Burke over to lean against the trunk of a tree while she did what he told her. Picking up the Uzi, Bethany was surprised by how lightweight it was. She'd never held one before, having only seen such weapons in movies and on TV. Getting it comfortably positioned and ready in her left hand, Bethany returned to Agent Burke. He heaved himself onto her again, arm around her shoulders, and together they got ready to move.

"Which way?" Bethany asked.

"Got any bars on your cell?" Agent Burke asked.

"I can't exactly check it holding you and this gun, ya know?" she answered snidely.

"Fair point," Agent Burke conceded and weakly raised a finger to point to the east. "We'll head over to the next search grid and hope we run into some of the others. If we're lucky, they should already be heading this way."

****

Manford ran through the woods. Each breath hurt like hell. The damned woman had shot him in the chest. His second skin was reinforced and usually could stop a small caliber round. The witch had fired point blank though and one of her first three shots had gotten through. Cursing his luck and his stupidity in being overconfident. Everything just kept going to crap.

He tasted blood in his mouth and knew it was his own. The woman had also fired two more rounds at him as he retreated. One of those missed entirely but the other had hit his back. The bullet hadn't penetrated his second skin but even so it must have left one hell of a bruise, maybe even cracking the rear side of one of his ribs because it hurt with every move he made. He didn't have any option but to keep running. If he stopped, the cops and agents after him would surely overwhelm him with their numbers and guns. It was a minor miracle that he was able to inflict the kind of damage on them that he had already. The tough, freaking sheriff was dead. That was no small feat. And Agent Burke, that bastard, was messed up badly. Badly enough that Manford figured the FBI agent would be forced to break off from the search himself in order to get medical attention. With the local sheriff and Agent Burke taken out, his odds of making it out of these woods alive and not in handcuffs had increased dramatically. They were the brains behind the manhunt. Without them there organizing things and holding it all together, slipping away from his pursuers would be a lot easier.

The huge right foot of his suit came down wrong amid a cluster of roots that were protruding upwards from the ground. Nearly breaking his ankle in the process, Manford cried out, flopping into the trunk of the tree the roots belonged to and then bouncing from it to land roughly on his hands. His breaths were sharp, wheezing noises now.

"Fragging hell!" Manford yelled. Doing so caused him even more pain. Sucking in a wheezing breath, a shudder ran through him. His vision blurred. Manford shook his head, trying to clear it, then remained where he was, waiting for the nausea rising within him to pass.

The bullet in his chest had done much more damage than he first thought. He needed help as much as that bastard FBI agent he had mangled did. The problem was that there was no one he could turn to for it. Manford doubted, even if he somehow doubled back and managed to get to his van, his equipment and medical gear there would be enough to help. He wasn't a doctor but certainly knew his way around the human body and tools used to open it up and patch it closed. From how he felt, the bullet surely was in his lung. He was living on borrowed time.

Slowly, painfully, Manford gripped the trunk of the tree next to him and used it to pull himself up. Manford stood there, wheezing, wondering just what in the hell he was going to do. A slight noise he couldn't fully identify made Manford raise his head and look around. His breath caught in his throat and his eyes bugged in their sockets. He blinked but they were still there.

Manford wondered if he was dying. That was what crossed his mind first. Was he just hallucinating from his exhaustion and wounds or had his brethren come to escort him into the great forest of the afterlife? His eyes had to be playing tricks on him. They just had to. What he saw couldn't be real, could it?

There were seven of them. The tallest had to be almost nine feet tall. The smallest was around seven feet in height. All of them were just like Manford always imagined Sasquatch would be. They were covered in brownish hair that blended in with the woods surrounding them. Their arms were overly long like a primate's. Their eyes, some pairs were yellow, others red. Manford couldn't explain the difference. He had no idea what it meant, if anything. . .and to be honest, he didn't care. All that mattered were that the Sasquatch were there, right there in front of him, around him, and truly real.

"My family," Manford said, a hand pressed to his chest, applying pressure to the bullet hole beneath his second skin. "I knew I would find you someday."

Tears welled up in Manford's eyes and flowed freely along the curves of his cheeks. "My brothers. . ." he sobbed, voice full of passion and relief. "Have you come to save me?"

The great beasts made no response. They merely stood watching him.

Manford raised himself up to his full height which was increased by his second skin. Sweat beaded on his skin inside his Sasquatch suit. He took pride in just how much it resembled the creatures. His lips parted in a smile. Extending a hand to the beasts, he said, "My brothers. . .my brothers. I have searched for you for so long."

The largest of the Sasquatch stepped closer. It towered over Manford. His wet eyes looked up into its face with a reverent love and awe. He was still smiling as the Sasquatch's clawed hand raked across the face of his second skin. The claws tore it to pieces, exposing Manford's sweaty true face, beady eyes, and wide smile. Manford backpedaled from the hulking beast. His smile fell away, Manford's elation turning to stark terror.

"Why?" he rasped, "Why?"

His voice rose into a frightened squeal. "I am one of you! I may look human but I am one of you! My father was one of you!"

Manford couldn't bring himself to strike back at the Sasquatch with his razor blade claws. His hands instead rose, open palmed, in a desperate gesture of surrender and appeasement.

The Sasquatch closed the distance Manford had tried to put between them with a single stride. Manford's pleading eyes met those of the beast. In them, he saw his death. It broke the serial killer at the very core of his being. He snapped in an outburst of rage born of grief and betrayal. Launching himself at the huge Sasquatch, Manford attacked with his metal claws, swinging wildly. The Sasquatch effortlessly dodged his maddened slashes, stepping just out of his reach. Manford, having failed, dropped to his knees, sobbing. Blood rose from his throat, bubbling out of his lips. Each breath sent an intense wave of pain coursing through him. Once again, his vision blurred. The distorted world swam before his tear filled eyes. He looked up at the Sasquatch. Manford took its stern gaze as one of pity and disgust. The Sasquatch drew close again. Its massive hands came to rest on the sides of Manford's head, cradling it gently. The emotional hurt was far worse than the pain raging through his body.

"Please," Manford whimpered weakly. "Please. I am one of you."

And those were his last words.

The Sasquatch twisted its hold on Manford. His neck snapped, breaking with a sharp crack, before his head was ripped away from where it sat upon his shoulders. A geyser of blood sprayed from the stump that remained atop his body, soaking the Sasquatch's hair with red. Manford's corpse toppled over. The huge Sasquatch moved aside as the others approached. Together they stomped on the serial killer until his body was nothing more than a smear of crushed entrails spilt over the grass and dirt. When that was finished, the huge leader of the beasts raised Manford's head to examine it. Then with a snarl, its thumbs sank into Manford's eye sockets. It wrenched Manford's skull apart in an explosion of gore and brain matter.

****

Bethany and Agent Burke moved through the trees at the fastest speed they could manage given the FBI agent's wounds. Burke's face was tough to look at so Bethany had jury rigged a bandage to at least wrap around his head to cover his mangled eye and nose. She couldn't get the sight of it out her head.

Something was rushing through the woods ahead of them. Bethany leveled the Uzi she was carrying at the noise.

"Wait!" Agent Burke stopped her from opening fire, slapping the barrel of the submachine gun down.

The noise was caused by the lead deputy, Frank, Steven, and the old man, Gary. As they came into view, a wave of relief surged through Bethany.

"Sir!" Steven shouted, rushing to Agent Burke. He took Burke's weight off of Bethany, helping the senior agent gently to the ground.

As Steven examined Agent Burke's wounds, Gary spat out a mouthful of tobacco juice and grumbled, "What the hell happened to him?"

"Manford," Bethany said the name of the

serial killer in a voice as cold and hard as ice.

Steven wasn't a medic but did have enough medical knowledge to be able to properly assess Agent Burke's condition. From his expression, Bethany could see that it wasn't as bad as she'd feared.

"We haven't been able to reach anyone else by radio or cell," Steven said as he finished looking Agent Burke over and craned his head around to look at her with worried eyes.

"Don't tell me we're the only ones. . ." Bethany stammered.

Agent Burke was nodding. "We have to assume that we are."

"Where's Sheriff Clark?" Frank asked, glaring at him.

"Dead," Agent Burke answered. "Manford got him."

"Damn it!" Frank punched the trunk of a tree. The act tore the knuckles of his right hand to shreds. He shook it, flinging drops of blood that splattered onto the grass.

"We can't allow Manford to escape," Agent Burke reminded everyone.

"Yeah," Frank huffed. "And just how in the hell are we supposed to stop him? We can't even find the bastard! He's been the one finding us out here!"

"We'll get more help," Agent Burke snapped. "Whatever it takes! We have to!"

"I'm not sure you're thinking clearly, Burke," Frank shot back.

"Steven," Agent Burke motioned for the tech to help him onto his feet.

"Ain't no sign of my dogs," Gary complained, "Ain't no sign of any of the other dogs either. They've all just vanished to God knows where."

"Dogs are smart," Bethany said. "Sometimes smarter than us. I'm sure they've all gotten the hell out of these woods and are safe back at the campground."

Gary shrugged and gave an unconcerned grunt. She knew the old man didn't care about his dogs like most handlers. To him, doing what they did was just a job. If his dogs got lost or hurt, Gary didn't care beyond how it impacted him and his wallet.

The two groups combined into a single one, Frank and Bethany watching the woods nervously as they made their way towards the campground.

"You stop to think that maybe it wasn't Manford who took out the other search groups?" Frank challenged Agent Burke.

The FBI agent frowned. "It was Manford that

killed your sheriff."

"That don't mean crap, Burke," Frank shook his head. "And you know it. The others could have easily been taken out by. . ."

"By what?" Gary was smirking. "Those creatures you people say are out here? That's a load of bull. Ain't nothing out here but us and the sicko killer."

Agent Burke was regretting not allowing the dog handlers to see the body of the monster Frank had killed. Before he could say anything to the grumpy old man, Frank let loose on Gary. The lead deputy grabbed Gary by the front of his shirt and shoved him up against a tree.

"Now you listen here, man," Frank growled, "I watched one of those things kill a friend of mine, you old fool. They are real and they are out here. You can stake your life on that. Fast, strong, giant things that are hard as hell to kill. And for all we know, they could be stalking us right now. You got that?"

"Sure, sure," Gary mumbled, frightened by Frank's outburst and roughness. "Whatever you say, Deputy. I didn't mean nothing by what I said. Honest."

"Just get your damn head in the game, Gary." Frank released his hold on the old man. "We're in danger every second we're out here and from more than just Manford. I need you sharp and focused."

"Yeah," Gary nodded. "I got it."

"Good," Frank worked the pump of the shotgun he carried, as if for dramatic effect, making sure a round was ready in its chamber. "Because one of those things could come at us at any second."

Bethany got the vibe that the old man didn't really believe Frank. It didn't matter though because the lead deputy had put Gary in his place and the old man was doing as he was told.

She was glad that Agent Burke was moving on his own again, some of his shock having passed. Steven kept close by his side. Frank was on point, leading the group's way and Gary brought up the rear, putting as much distance as possible between himself and Frank.

Agent Burke hadn't taken his Uzi from her. Bethany held onto it. The compact submachine gun brought her some comfort. Glancing up, Bethany noticed that the sun, long past its zenith in the sky now, was beginning its slow descent. She wanted to yell at the others that they needed to hurry. Her gut told Bethany that something even worse than what they had already been through was coming when the sun went down and darkness fell.

She wondered where Manford was. There was no sign of the serial killer since he'd killed Sheriff Clark and she shot him, point blank. His freaky Sasquatch suit might have stopped the bullets she fired from hurting him but then again, as close as they had been, it might not have. She hoped the bastard was bleeding to death out there somewhere.

An inhuman roar echoed through the trees.

"What the. . .?" Gary squeaked.

"Everybody hold up!" Frank shouted. "Eyes on the trees!"

The group stopped, drawing closer to each other.

"What was that?" Bethany asked.

"It sure as hell wasn't the serial killer you folks are chasing," Gary said. "Wasn't no animal either. I've been coming out to these woods since I was knee high and I ain't never heard anything like that."

"Shut up!" Frank barked. His gaze swept the area around them.

"It's one of them," Agent Burke spoke up, "isn't it?"

Agent Burke knew that Frank was the one who killed the monster Sheriff Clark had shown him. His instincts and logic told him that the beast wasn't the only one of its kind no matter how much Agent Burke hoped it was just an aberration. Sheriff Clark had thought it was just a kid and that its parents would be even larger and more vicious than how Frank described the thing.

"What do we do?" Bethany whispered to Frank.

"Try to stay alive," the lead deputy snapped at her.

The woods were quiet. The group listened with baited breath, waiting, to see if anything was coming their way. Bethany could see that Frank and the young forensic tech, Steven, were scared out of their minds despite the front they were both trying to put up. Agent Burke merely looked resolved to accept whatever was about to happen with a stoic, hard expression on his blood-smeared, half bandage-covered face. Gary chewed on his tobacco and held the hunting rifle he carried ready. Bethany's palms were slick with sweat against the metal of the Uzi in her hands.

"I think we're clear," Gary said to no one in particular.

Frank was shaking his head.

"No. We're not," Agent Burke warned.

"Look!" Bethany yelled and pointed in its direction as she saw the beast. As scary as

Manford's suit was, this thing was way worse. It stood over eight feet tall and almost completely blended in with the woods around it. The thing was covered head to toe in thick brownish hair. Its eyes were full of feral rage and the yellow teeth that were exposed by its snarl gleamed in the dying rays of the setting sun. The beast was just standing amid the growing shadows, watching them.

"Nobody move," Agent Burke ordered.

Frank wasn't having it though. He'd faced one of the beasts before and knew how fast and deadly such creatures could be. His shotgun came up and thundered. The round he fired missed the hulking beast. The Sasquatch sprang into motion, dodging the heavy slug which struck the trunk of a tree, sending splinters erupting from it.

"What the hell?" Gary shouted, unable to believe something so large could move so fast even seeing it with his own eyes.

The Sasquatch sped through the woods, emerging from them to the group's right. It came out roaring, plowing straight into Steven and swept him up from the ground. With a ferocious yank, the Sasquatch ripped away the young tech's arms in an explosion of gore. Steven's armless form flopped down at the Sasquatch's feet as the beast tossed away his arms in different directions. The hulking monster had left itself open in that moment. Frank made use of it. His shotgun boomed as he pulled its trigger. A hole was punched in the beast's chest. Frank worked the pump of his shotgun chambering another round but didn't need to. Bethany, of all people, had stepped forward to join the battle. The Uzi in her hands blazed away at the Sasquatch cutting a streak of mangled red across its mid-section. Its abdomen opened up, the Sasquatch's guts spilled out from the long wound, folds of severed flesh peeling outward, as red-slicked, purple snakes splattered and coiled wetly between its legs in the grass. The Sasquatch gave a whimper, its hair-covered hands moving to clamp onto its stomach, holding in the rest of its bowels.

Gary, taking aim at the injured beast's head with his rifle, ended it. His high powered rifle cracked, kicking against his shoulder where it was braced. The Sasquatch's head was knocked backwards atop its neck as the bullet entered its forehead. The rear side of its skull shattered as a spray of bone fragments, brain matter, and blood accompanied the bullet in its exit. The Sasquatch toppled, thudding onto the ground.

"Yeehah!" Gary whooped. "Take that, you

mother!"

"Stow it!" Frank snapped as the deputy saw that their fight wasn't over. Another creature was bounding in their direction, breaking low lying tree branches as it came, a charging juggernaut of raw, primal power. Bethany spun towards the new threat, squeezing the trigger of the Uzi. The submachine gun clicked empty.

"Here!" Agent Burke tossed the dog handler a fresh magazine. As she scrambled to reload, it was up to Frank and Gary to stop the monster and they were trying.

Frank's shotgun boomed and Gary's rifle cracked. The Sasquatch was even larger than the beast they'd just killed. This thing stood over nine feet tall. It took their fire head on, allowing the shotgun blast to tear at its shoulder and the rifle round to graze the side of its neck without even attempting to dodge them. Its eyes were ablaze with a burning rage. Running straight up to the two men, the fingers of a hair-covered hand closed around Gary's throat as its other hand slapped Frank so hard that the lead deputy was sent crashing into the trunk of a tree. Frank bounced off of it, body rolling, to come to a stop several feet away. The lead deputy lay there, either unconscious or dead, as Gary struggled to break free. His legs scissored beneath him, kicking at the Sasquatch. The beast didn't even seem to feel the blows they dealt it. Jerking Gary's head to its mouth, the Sasquatch bit deeply into the front of his face. As it pulled away, there was a ragged, bloody hole where Gary's nose had been. He made horrid, wet sounds, as the Sasquatch chewed upon what its teeth had taken from him.

Bethany managed to eject the Uzi's spent magazine, fumbling another into the weapon. She readied the submachine gun and looked up from her efforts to realize that Gary was dead. The Sasquatch tossed his corpse aside, locking its yellow gaze onto her.

Agent Burke grabbed the Uzi from her, shoving Bethany aside as the Sasquatch came snarling towards where they stood. The Uzi bucked in his hands as Agent Burke poured a stream of fully automatic fire into the Sasquatch's groin. His thinking was that was the softest, most easily hurt area of the monster's hulking form. He was right. The Sasquatch shrieked in pain, tripping up, and fell forward, carried on by its momentum to come half bouncing, half rolling at Burke, end over end. The FBI agent had no time to dodge. It struck him like a runaway eighteen wheeler. Agent Burke felt his right leg break and then bounce on past him. Howling in pain, Agent Burke twisted his body, to get the barrel of his Uzi pointed at the monster as it finally crashed into the bottom of a tree. As the Sasquatch raised its head to look back at Burke, black lips parted in a snarl that promised vengeance, he emptied the remainder of the magazine into its face. Both of the Sasquatch's eyes were reduced to pulp in their sockets as bullets ripped away the hair and flesh that covered cheek bones. The Sasquatch made an attempt to get up but failed.

Bethany, having watched it all helplessly, spotted Gary's rifle in the grass and ran to get it.

"Finish the bastard off!" Agent Burke grunted through the grimace of pain that was on his face.

She worked the lever of the high powered rifle as she walked up to the thrashing form of the badly wounded beast. Lowering the rifle's barrel, Bethany fired into the top of its head at point blank range. The Sasquatch was abruptly silenced and fell still.

"We've got to get the hell out of here before more of those things show up," Agent Burke yelled. "Help me!"

"I gotta check on Frank!" she responded, heading to where the lead deputy lay sprawled out. Kneeling next to him, Bethany stuck two fingers to the side of his throat feeling for a pulse. "He's alive."

"Great," Agent Burke said snidely. "You can't carry both of us."

Torn as to what to do, Bethany froze up. She didn't want to leave either of the two men to die.

"Now get your butt over here and help me, damn it," Agent Burke ordered. "We'll come back for him."

Bethany prayed inwardly that there weren't any more of the Sasquatch among the trees surrounding them and that Frank would be fine until they could get help as she rushed to take Agent Burke's hand. She heaved, yanking him up. Agent Burke screamed as pain set fire to the nerves in his broken leg. Looking down at it, Bethany could see the jagged white of bone sticking out through the red-soaked cloth of his pants. It nearly caused her to vomit at the sight of it. Agent Burke went limp in her arms as she strained to support his weight. He recovered in just enough time to keep them both from teetering over. She got his arm better positioned around her shoulders and they started hobbling along again in the direction of the campground that was being used as their basecamp.

"You sure you're going to be able to make it?" Bethany asked, not seeing how the FBI agent could endure what had to be utter torture with each step they took together.

Agent Burke was about to tell Bethany to shut the hell up and move but as they took their next step together, there was a crunching sound within his broken leg. He screamed at the top of his lungs and his vision darkened. Agent Burke heard Bethany yelling at him but a sea of darkness arose and swallowed him.

Bethany grunted, twisting her body, doing all she could to lower the FBI agent down as gently as she could. Even with giving it everything she had Agent Burke still dropped roughly enough to the ground to break his leg even more. It was nearly separated between his knee and groin. It looked as if the pants he wore more than anything was all that was keeping the leg in place.

"Oh Lord," Bethany croaked, jerking her eyes away from the grisly sight.

Agent Burke was out but still breathing. She could see the rise and fall of his labored breathing. Bethany backpedaled from where he lay in a state of panic. She was alone now and couldn't cope with it. A cry of terror erupted from Bethany, hands coming up to cover her mouth. Stumbling, one of her hands shot out to catch herself. Rough tree bark scraped away the skin of her palm.

"Damn it!" Bethany yelped as the shock of her injury brought her back to a rational state. Seeing Frank, Bethany knew what she had to do. Pouncing towards him, she slapped the hell out of him. Sucking in a sharp breath, Frank came awake.

The lead deputy took a swing at her from where he lay in the grass. Bethany narrowly avoided getting clobbered by his fist.

"Whoa!" Bethany cried. "It's me, Frank! It's Bethany!"

"Bethany?" Frank asked, his eyes darting about as if the lead deputy was trying to figure out where he was. Then they suddenly went wide as if the memories of everything burst into his mind.

"Where's. . .?" Frank started.

"We killed the monster that hit you, another one too, Frank," Bethany explained. "But everyone else is dead except for Agent Burke. He passed out on me. One of his legs is. . .messed up pretty bad."

Frank sat up, seeming to come to his senses.

"That bastard sure packed a punch," he grunted, rubbing his chest where the Sasquatch's hand had struck him. Peeping down his shirt, Frank saw a huge purple bruise there. He took a breath, testing to see how bad it hurt to do. There were no sharp pains so Frank figured his ribs were okay. Heaving himself onto his feet, Frank quickly found his shotgun and made sure the weapon hadn't been damaged. It looked fine too.

"Agent Burke wanted me to leave you behind," Bethany told him. "If he hadn't passed out. . ."

"It's alright," Frank soothed her. "I would have done the same."

"So we're going to leave him?" Bethany asked.

The lead deputy nodded. "We need to move fast and he would only slow us down. The truth of the matter is we have no idea how many more of those things are out here. Even running into just one would be a fight. We run into a pack of them and it's game over. Someone has to make it to the campground and let the others know what's out here. With the Sheriff dead and Burke out of commission, Captain Slater of the state boys will be in charge."

"The state troopers," Bethany said, "I wonder if they've been attacked yet."

"We won't know anything until we reach the campground," Frank shrugged.

The sun was almost completely set. The

shadows grew deeper even as they hurried through the woods. They pushed as hard as they could. If they didn't reach the campground before night fully fell, well, Frank didn't want to think about that.

****

Frank and Bethany reached the campground ahead of sundown with over half an hour to spare. The scene was much as they left it except that the reporters were now gone. Captain Slater, apparently, hadn't put up with their crap. Frank knew that they couldn't be kept away forever. Parts of what was actually going on likely had already broke in the papers and on TV. The full story, that, with a bit of luck, might be kept quiet a tiny bit longer.

A pair of troopers met them as they came wandering in.

"You look like crap," one of them commented.

"What the hell happened to you?" another asked.

"Where's Slater?" Frank roared at them.

"Over there," the first trooper pointed deeper into the campground where a few of Agent Burke's forensic people were gathered about a van with a dish on top of it. Captain Slater was with them, talking adamantly about something.

Frank marched straight up to Captain Slater. Bethany followed a few steps behind, hanging back so as to not get in his way. Captain Slater's expression was a startled one at the sight of Frank approaching him.

"Deputy," Captain Slater eyed him. "You got something to say to me?"

"Sheriff Clark's dead. Agent Burke too," Frank's voice was hard and cold.

The state troopers' captain looked as if someone had punched him in the gut. His eyes went wide. "Dead?"

Captain Slater took a moment to recover before speaking again, "Manford got them? Both of them? Hellfire, is the bastard Superman or something?"

"Wasn't Manford. That bastard is dead too," Frank somewhat lied, bending the truth to strengthen his next words. "We got trouble coming."

Some of the FBI agents gathered about their communications van sucked in frightened breaths and gasped. All of them suddenly wore looks of grave concern. Frank knew Agent Burke had made sure his people knew about the things out in the woods.

"You just said that Manford was dead,

Deputy," Captain Slater frowned.

"Yeah," Frank nodded, "What killed him and the others is our trouble and they're almost certainly heading here right now."

Captain Slater's eyes hardened. "I don't understand."

"Did Sheriff Clark show you the body?" Frank asked.

Shaking his head, Captain Slater said, "I don't have a fragging clue what you're talking about, Frank."

"Come on then," the lead deputy told the state trooper captain. "You need to see it."

Frank led the captain to the van where Sheriff Clark had the small Sasquatch body stored, the one Frank had killed himself. He reached out and took hold of the handles to its rear doors.

"Just what you got in there?" Captain Slater half snickered.

"You wouldn't believe me," Frank sighed. "You just need to see it."

Frank opened the rear of the van. Captain Slater flinched as if a snake was striking at him. Frank couldn't blame him. The thing in the van shouldn't exist in the real world. It was more the stuff of nightmares and myths.

"Holy. . ." Captain Slater waved a hand in front of his face in a vain attempt to drive away the odors of heavy musk and decay that drifted out from the van's rear.

"That thing killed a friend of mine before I took it down," Frank told Slater. "It sure as hell wasn't easy to kill either."

"What is it?" Captain Slater stammered before he was able to recover his professional demeanor.

"It's a Sasquatch," Bethany intruded on the conversation.

"You're fragging messing with me," Captain Slater shook his head, not wanting to believe what his eyes were seeing and his nose smelling.

"We're not," Frank assured the captain. "That thing is real. Touch it if you need to but we aren't doing anything but telling you the truth."

"That thing is a Sasquatch and there are a hell of a lot more of the beasts in those woods," Bethany pointed at the trees at the edge of the campground.

"And they're ticked off now," Frank added. "We went into their turf, killed some of their family, and barely got out with our lives."

"I don't. . ." Captain Slater stared and realized he had no idea what to say.

"You can damn well bet they're coming, Captain," Frank told him. "And as soon as that sun goes down, they're going to hit us hard."

"Are you saying we need to pull out of here, Frank?" Captain Slater stared at the lead deputy.

"No, Slater," Frank met his eyes. "I am saying we need to get ready. This may be the only chance we ever get to take these things on out in the open. We need to stop them here and now, kill every last one of the fragging things. Your people need to be ready and you need to get on the horn. Call in the S.W.A.T. unit they got over in Asheville. I don't know that they can make it here in time but trust me, we'd rather have them on the way than not."

Captain Slater looked from Frank to Bethany and then back again.

"Alright, Frank," Captain Slater said, "I believe you. I'll make the call. You go on and start doing whatever you think needs to be done here."

Frank knew there was no chance of getting everyone to believe and no time to bring them all over to see the corpse in the van. The officers wouldn't understand what they were up against but at least they would be in position and ready to get the job done.

Bethany joined Frank in running about the campground, warning the officers to get ready, that they soon would be under attack. None of them would have listened to her but Agent

Burke's people backed her up. And it was easy to see that *they* were sure as hell taking her warning seriously. The handful of agents had brought out some serious firepower from their van. Some of them carried freaking M4 carbines and the rest Remington 870s in addition to the sidearms they'd strapped on.

Within minutes, the officers in the campground had formed an old school, defensive circle like in the days of the Old West. It was the best Frank and Bethany could whip them into. Frank had no intention of fighting a fully defensive battle though. He needed everyone in the clearing to be ready to switch from defense to offense as soon as the chance arose. Hell, Frank knew they would be lucky just to hold the line once the troopers saw what they were up against.

Frank stood in the center of the circle formed around the FBI communications van. Captain Slater emerged from it.

"It's done," he told Frank. "Asheville's S.W.A.T. team is en route. E.T.A in fifteen. I've called in some other help too that should be here ahead of them."

Frank glanced up at the darkening sky and grunted.

"In fifteen minutes, we might all be dead, so

let's hope whoever else you called gets here a lot faster," Frank commented.

"Come on now," Captain Slater challenged him. "Those things are just animals."

"Sure," Frank didn't argue. "Animals that are built like tanks, strong enough to rip a man apart down his middle, and can move like lightning."

"I get that they're real, Frank. I do," Captain Slater said, "but do you seriously think those things are that dangerous? Maybe what you saw out there in those woods. . ."

"I'm fine," Frank reached to pick up the M4 carbines one of the FBI agents had placed on the hood of the van for him and readied it. "And you're about to find out that I ain't overestimating those things in the least. If anything, I'm underplaying what we're about to be facing, Slater. That sun will be gone in just another minute or two and then. . .then you and your boys are going to find out exactly what hell is like."

****

Darkness fell. The earlier rain was gone but thick clouds remained, blotting out the stars. Beyond the campground, the night was pitch black. It wasn't. Captain Slater's people had set up lights all throughout the firing lines positioned behind the circled cars. Fingers waited on triggers and palms were wet with sweat as everyone waited for the things in the woods to show themselves. Frank's gut told him that it wouldn't be long until they did.

"I hope to God you're wrong about all this, Frank," Captain Slater said. "You know it's likely going to cost you your badge if you are."

Frank didn't acknowledge Captain Slater's somewhat veiled threat. Leaving Slater at the van, Frank walked to join the northward facing portion of the firing line. Bethany joined him there. He could see that she was upset. Her dogs were nowhere to be found. None of the other dogs were either. Not a single one of the animals had returned to the campground. That didn't mean the beasts had killed them. Frank hoped the dogs had gotten away and found their own way. He didn't waste the breath to share his hope with Bethany though. She would continue to worry about her dogs until either they came back or their bodies were found later on.

"I'm sorry," Frank said to Bethany.

Confused, she looked over at him where the two of them were crouched behind the hood of a patrol car.

"What for?" Bethany frowned.

"If it weren't for the sheriff and me," the

words were difficult for him to get out, "you would never have gotten dragged into all this."

"Frank," Bethany reached over to put a hand on his shoulder. "It's not your fault."

He pulled away from her touch.

"It's not," Bethany repeated. "We were all just doing our jobs and if we hadn't, no one would know that those things are out there."

Behind them, back at the FBI van's side door, Captain Slater was fuming. Both Sheriff Clark and that Burke jerk had known about the creatures that could be out there and hadn't told him squat. His officers had been out there, easy prey, for the beasts, with zero knowledge that they were in any danger. He'd worked with Sheriff Clark many times before and it truly bothered him to have been left out.

An FBI agent who went by the name Caz, with long blonde hair that was pulled into a tight ponytail that dangled down her back. She was quite a bit younger than he was. Captain Slater guessed Caz was likely in her late twenties. With Burke and the other lead agents missing, dead if Frank was telling the truth, Caz was the ranking FBI officer on the scene. Any who worked in what Captain Slater thought of as real law enforcement could easily see that Caz was a desk jockey. She was armed with an M4 carbine and clearly had some training with the weapon. Captain Slater very much doubted Caz had fired any type of weapon since that training though.

"You really believe there are more of those things out there?" he asked her.

"My boss did," Agent Caz answered. "That's enough for me. Agent Burke very seldom made mistakes."

"That so?" Captain Slater challenged her. "Then why wasn't Manford already behind bars instead of in Sheriff Clark's town adding to his victim list?"

"Manford was special," Agent Caz shifted the M4 into a more comfortable position in her hands. "We're standing here talking about that sicko like we know he's dead but we don't, do we? All we have is the word of a deputy whose mental and emotional states are questionable. For all we know, Manford is out there with those beasts that are supposedly coming for us."

"That's hardly an answer to what I asked," Captain Slater smirked.

"Agent Burke was one of the best. There's no question about that but Manford. . .like I said, Manford was special. He was one of those serial killers that only comes around once in a decade or more. Manford was Moriarty to Burke's Holmes. That's the best I can explain it. The two of them were just too evenly matched for either of them to get the better of the other without some luck."

Captain Slater grunted and changed the subject.

"You're good with Frank's plan?" he asked.

"It's as good a plan as any if we're trying to wipe these things out," Agent Caz sighed. "We let them come to us, give them a break in the lines, then encircle them and pour enough bullets into the things to turn them into bloody smears on the grass."

"It sounds even crazier when somebody says it out loud," Captain Slater frowned as he had been going over and over the plan in his head.

"What worries me is how tough that deputy claims these things are," Agent Caz said. "If they're all he says they are, I don't think we're going to need to give them a way inside our lines. They'll break through on their own and we may find ourselves utterly screwed when they do."

"We are sure as hell going to need to save their bodies because there's no way anyone is ever going to believe any of this without them," Captain Slater commented.

"Ha," Agent Caz grinned. "I'll agree with that."

"Look at him," Captain Slater gestured at Frank where the lead deputy crouched, waiting for the beasts to arrive. "I've known Frank for a while. Long enough to see that running into those things has changed him."

"For better or worse?" Agent Caz asked.

"I guess we'll see, won't we?" Captain Slater shrugged.

****

The minutes ticked by like hours. Frank watched the tree line over the hood of the car he and Bethany were using as cover. He knew the beasts were out there. Frank could feel it in his bones. So what in the hell were they waiting on? Night had fallen and the woods were nothing more than a sea of deep shadows. The circle of vehicles where Frank and his people were ready to make their stand was an island of light in the darkness. A pair of huge floodlights swept back and forth over the tree line, one to the north and the other to the south. Their beams chased away the darkness at the edge of the trees but still, there was nothing to see. Not so much as a single sign of the beasts.

Bethany clutched the shotgun she had been armed with so tightly that her knuckles were white. Her every muscle was tensed up. It was like waiting for the world to end. Counting all the FBI agents and state troopers, there were over two dozen officers inside the large circle of vehicles. They had numbers, at least Bethany hoped that was true, and a massive amount of firepower to bring to bear on the Sasquatch. The beasts shouldn't have much of a chance as long as there were only a few of them. Yet, her stomach churned.

"Frank, if we live through this. . ." Bethany's words trailed off as she saw the beasts. They were at the edge of the woods but still far enough back in the trees to effectively engage. Inwardly she chuckled. *Effectively engage*, she thought, am I living in an SF novel now? Her mirth died as quickly as it had been born as one of the beasts out there loosed a thunderous roar.

The beasts came bounding from the woods to the north. There was dozens of them, all raging and howling. They varied in sizes from slightly over seven feet tall to nine foot, hulking giants. Their eyes glowed yellow and red in the darkness.

Frank noticed several of the beasts lingering at the tree line. They didn't charge out with the others. At their center was the largest of the beasts. It stood ten feet tall and was unquestionably the leader or chief.

The state troopers and federal agents opened fire. The cacophony of fully automatic M4A1s and booming shotguns was deafening. The fastest of the Sasquatch squealed and shrieked as their bodies were ripped and torn by the barrage of bullets and slugs that met them. One Sasquatch's chest was nothing more than a ragged mess of red that resembled ground up beef as it fell. Another of the beasts took a shotgun slug to its mouth that caved in its teeth. A flap of flesh dangled where its left cheek had been, the white of bone clearly visible.

Bethany aimed her shot as best she could. The shotgun braced against her shoulder bucked as she fired. The shot blew apart the kneecap of a Sasquatch. Howling in pain, the great beast tumbled, rolling and bouncing, carried forward by its own momentum.

Next to her, Frank's M4A1 chattered in short bursts. A Sasquatch's roar was turned into a sickening gargle as bullets punched through its throat. Quickly swinging his carbine to target another of the beasts, Frank aimed for its groin, firing a trio of short bursts into it. The Sasquatch wailed, a high pitched shriek. Blood splattered from between the beast's legs as everything there was shredded. The Sasquatch fell to its knees, eyes rolling upwards in its head, and collapsed the rest of the way to the ground, face first.

The state troopers and federal agents who had never faced the great beasts before weren't aiming their fire as carefully as Frank and Bethany. Their training told them to go for body shots and count on the sheer amount of fire to bring down the beasts. That worked too but nowhere near as well. Many of the beasts were merely slowed by the barrage hammering them. Others weren't hit at all as their brothers and sisters around them were. A full third of the charging Sasquatch reached the circle of vehicles. Frank watched as an eight foot tall beast with shaggy gray hair covering its body leaped on top of a patrol car. Glass blew outward from its windows as the roof caved in from its weight. A state trooper was sprayed by it. Pieces slashed at the skin of his cheeks, leaving red trails, but it was a large shard that went tip first into his throat that killed him. A trooper next to him jerked his shotgun up to take a shot at the Sasquatch on top of the car but it jumped down onto him, ripping the weapon from his grasp, taking his trigger finger away with it. The trooper opened his mouth to scream but the Sasquatch, moving impossibly fast, grabbed the man and rammed his head into the side of the patrol car. The bone of his skull crunched and broke. The Sasquatch flung his corpse aside. Frank knew he had to stop the monster. Getting up from his place on the firing line, he rushed it, emptying his M4A1's magazine into the beast as he ran. Most of his hurried shots struck the beast's upper chest with little to no effect beyond making it angrier. With no time to reload, Frank let the carbine fall from his hands as the huge beast sprang forward to meet him. Drawing the .44 Magnum holstered on his belt with the skill and speed of an Old West gunfighter, Frank aimed for the great beast's forehead. He missed, the bullet striking the upper portion of its nose instead. Still the shot was enough to hurt and stun the Sasquatch. It staggered as Frank closed in to fire another shot at point blank range into the same spot his first hit. The Sasquatch's head snapped back as the bullet entered its brain.

"Look out!" Frank heard Bethany shouting.

He spun to see another Sasquatch coming at him at a full out sprint. It plowed straight into the patrol car that was between them, pushing it inward and separating it from the cars parked on either side of it. Metal crumpled and crunched from the impact. Frank threw himself to the right, barely dodging the snarling Sasquatch's first swing at him. Its second grazed his left shoulder, dislocating it. A sharp grunt escaped Frank. Gritting his teeth against the pain, Frank stayed on his feet. The Sasquatch would have finished him in that moment but Bethany saved his life. From seemingly out of nowhere, she was there, between him and the monster. Her shotgun boomed. The heavy slug Bethany fired punched into the Sasquatch's chest. It reacted by swinging both of its hands in mighty, sweeping arcs, to bring them together on Bethany's head which exploded like an over ripe melon hit by a sledgehammer. Bloody gore and Bethany's brain matter splashed over Frank.

"No!" he heard himself screaming as Bethany's headless body flopped to the ground and lay there twitching.

Frank rushed the huge beast, shoving the barrel of his .44 upwards, underneath its chin, metal slipping through hair, and pulled the trigger. The top of the Sasquatch's skull was blown away as the large caliber round ripped through it.

The battle was dying down. Most of the gunfire had fallen silent replaced by the sounds of men crying out and flesh being rended, torn, and gnawed upon. Frank saw that the few, scattered survivors among the troopers and federal agents weren't going to last much longer.

He saw that Captain Slater was dead. A tree limb that one of the Sasquatch had used like a spear impaled his chest, pinning him to the communications van. Seeing Slater, Frank knew they had lost. The beasts were just too tough and fast for them to have ever really stood a chance.

Frank heard them before he saw them. The two Ah-64E National Guard attack helicopters swept in, glorious and deadly before his eyes. Hellfire missiles flew from the launchers on their sides, leaving tracers of smoke in the night sky. They struck in the edge of the tree line where the largest of the Sasquatch still remained. Fire and splintering wood erupted upwards and outward as the missiles detonated.

"Get down!" Frank yelled at the few other survivors. He dove for cover himself as the Apaches came to a stop in the air, hovering to where their 30mm M230E1 chain guns blazed. The Sasquatch in and around the circle of vehicles met their ends, some nearly vaporized by the fury of the Apaches' attack.

Cheers went up from the survivors. The half a dozen Sasquatch that were still alive made a run for the trees but the attack copters weren't having it. They maneuvered to sweep in and finish them.

And just like that, it was all over.

Frank fell to his knees, thanking God that he was alive when so many others weren't.

EPILOGUE

Three months had passed since the battle of Green Grove Campground. The National Guard had searched the surrounding woods and mountains hunting for more of the Sasquatch only to find nothing. After two weeks, the units had been recalled and the area declared clear of the beasts and safe once more.

Most everything of what actually had happened was kept from or rather distorted to the press. The whole thing was played off as a chemical spill which led to a series of explosions that claimed the lives of Sheriff Clark and all the others who were taking part in the manhunt for a serial killer.

Frank had started smoking. The ashtray on his desk was full of discarded butts as he sucked smoke from the first cigarette of his second pack of the day into his lungs. He was currently serving as interim Sheriff and very likely to permanently get the job in the weeks to come. While the National Guard did their sweep, he'd been busy restaffing his force. New deputies, young and old, filled the department. The mayor and council had agreed to increase the department's budget and as thus Frank was able to double its size.

He rarely slept well. His dreams were nightmares haunted by the snarling, parted black lips of hungry Sasquatch. Despite having been told that the beasts were all dead, Frank couldn't bring himself to believe that, making sure his deputies were never on patrol alone and that outlying places like the remains of Green Grove campground were regularly checked for signs of the beasts. So far, nothing had been found by his people either but deep down, Frank knew, one day, the Sasquatch would return. They were the masters of hiding after all...he was sure more of them were out there, biding their time, waiting on the perfect night to extract their vengeance.

The End

Eric S Brown is the author of numerous book series including the Bigfoot War series, the Psi-Mechs Inc. series, the Kaiju Apocalypse series (with Jason Cordova), the Crypto-Squad series (with Jason Brannon), the Jack Bunny Bam series, and the A Pack of Wolves series. Some of his stand alone books include Snarl, Sasquatch Nightmare, Manhunt, Cryptid Park, War of the Worlds plus Blood Guts and Zombies, Casper Alamo (with Jason Brannon), Sasquatch Island, Day of the Sasquatch, Bigfoot, Crashed, World War of the Dead, Last Stand in a Dead Land, Sasquatch Lake, Kaiju Armageddon, Megalodon, Megalodon Apocalypse, Kraken, Alien Battalion, The Last Fleet, and From the Snow They Came to name only a few. His short fiction has been published hundreds of times in the small press in beyond including markets like the Onward Drake and Black Tide Rising anthologies from Baen Books, the Grantville Gazette, the SNAFU Military horror anthology series, and Walmart World magazine. He has done the novelizations for such films as Boggy Creek: The Legend is True (Studio 3 Entertainment) and The Bloody Rage of Bigfoot (Great Lake films). The first book of his Bigfoot War series was adapted into a feature film by Origin Releasing in 2014. Werewolf Massacre at Hell's Gate was the second of his books to be adapted into film in 2015. Major Japanese publisher, Takeshobo, bought the reprint rights to his Kaiju Apocalypse series (with Jason Cordova) and the mass market, Japanese language version was released in late 2017. Ring of Fire Press has released a collected edition of his Monster Society stories (set in the New York Times Best-selling world of Eric Flint's 1632). In addition to his fiction, Eric also wrote a pop culture column featured in Altered Reality Magazine for many years. Eric lives in North Carolina with his wife and two children where he continues to write tales of the hungry dead, blazing guns, and the things that lurk in the woods.

Check out other great
Cryptid Novels!

P.K. Hawkins
THE CRYPTID FILES

Fresh out of the academy with top marks, Agent Bradley Tennyson is expecting to have the pick of cases and investigations throughout the country. So he's shocked when instead he is assigned as the new partner to "The Crag," an agent well past his prime. He thinks the assignment is a punishment. It's anything but. Agent George Crag has been doing this job for far longer than most, and he knows what skeletons his bosses have in the closet and where the bodies are buried. He has pretty much free reign to pick his cases, and he knows exactly which one he wants to use to break in his new young partner: the disappearance and murder of a couple of college kids in a remote mountain town. Tennyson doesn't realize it, but Crag is about to introduce him to a world he never believed existed: The Cryptid Files, a world of strange monsters roaming in the night. Because these murders have been going on for a long time, and evidence is mounting that the murderer may just in fact be the legendary Bigfoot.

Gerry Griffiths
DOWN FROM BEAST MOUNTAIN

A beast with a grudge has come down from the mountain to terrorize the townsfolk of Porterville. The once sleepy town is suddenly wide awake. Sheriff Abel McGuire and game warden Grant Tanner frantically investigate one brutal slaying after another as they follow the blood trail they hope will eventually lead to the monstrous killer. But they better hurry and stop the carnage before the census taker has to come out and change the population sign on the edge of town to ZERO.

Check out other great

Cryptid Novels!

Hunter Shea

LOCH NESS REVENGE

Deep in the murky waters of Loch Ness, the creature known as Nessie has returned. Twins Natalie and Austin McQueen watched in horror as their parents were devoured by the world's most infamous lake monster. Two decades later, it's their turn to hunt the legend. But what lurks in the Loch is not what they expected. Nessie is devouring everything in and around the Loch, and it's not alone. Hell has come to the Scottish Highlands. In a fierce battle between man and monster, the world may never be the same. Praise for THEY RISE : "Outrageous, balls to the wall...made me yearn for 3D glasses and a tub of popcorn, extra butter!" – The Eyes of Madness "A fast-paced, gore-heavy splatter fest of sharksploitation." The Werd "A rocket paced horror story. I enjoyed the hell out of this book." Shotgun Logic Reviews

C.G. Mosley

BAKER COUNTY BIGFOOT CHRONICLE

Marie Bledsoe only wants her missing brother Kurt back. She'll stop at nothing to make it happen and, with the help of Kurt's friend Tony, along with Sheriff Ray Cochran, Marie embarks on a terrifying journey deep into the belly of the mysterious Walker Laboratory to find him. However, what she and her companions find lurking in the laboratory basement is beyond comprehension. There are cryptids from the forest being held captive there and something...else. Enjoy this suspenseful tale from the mind of C.G. Mosley, author of Wood Ape. Welcome back to Baker County, a place where monsters do lurk in the night!

Check out other great
Cryptid Novels!

Hunter Shea
THE DOVER DEMON

The Dover Demon is real...and it has returned. In 1977, Sam Brogna and his friends came upon a terrifying, alien creature on a deserted country road. What they witnessed was so bizarre, so chilling, they swore their silence. But their lives were changed forever. Decades later, the town of Dover has been hit by a massive blizzard. Sam's son, Nicky, is drawn to search for the infamous cryptid, only to disappear into the bowels of a secret underground lair. The Dover Demon is far deadlier than anyone could have believed. And there are many of them. Can Sam and his reunited friends rescue Nicky and battle a race of creatures so powerful, so sinister, that history itself has been shaped by their secretive presence? "THE DOVER DEMON is Shea's most delightful and insidiously terrifying monster yet." – Shotgun Logic Reviews "An excellent horror novel and a strong standout in the UFO and cryptid subgenres." –Hellnotes "Non-stop action awaits those brave enough to dive into the small town of Dover, and if you're lucky, you won't see the Demon himself!" – The Scary Reviews PRAISE FOR SWAMP MONSTER MASSACRE "B-horror movie fans rejoice, Hunter Shea is here to bring you the ultimate tale of terror!" – Horror Novel Reviews "A nonstop thrill ride! I couldn't put this book down." – Cedar Hollow Horror Reviews

Armand Rosamilia
THE BEAST

The end of summer, 1986. With only a few days left until the new school year, twins Jeremy and Jack Schaffer are on very different paths. Jeremy is the geek, playing Dungeons & Dragons with friends Kathleen and Randy, while Jack is the jock, getting into trouble with his buddies. And then everything changes when neighbor Mister Higgins is killed by a wild animal in his yard. Was it a bear? There's something big lurking in the woods behind their New Jersey home. Will the police be able to solve the murder before more Middletown residents are ripped apart?